THE MIDDLE AGES COME TO LIFE . . .
TO BRING US MURDER

THE SISTER FREVISSE MYSTERIES
by Margaret Frazer

THE NOVICE'S TALE

Among the nuns at St. Frideswide were piety, peace, and a little vial of poison . . .

"Frazer uses her extensive knowledge of the period to create an unusual plot . . . appealing characters and crisp writing."
—*Los Angeles Times*

"A fast-paced and seamless story."
—*St. Paul Pioneer-Express*

THE SERVANT'S TALE
Nominated for the Edgar Award

A troupe of actors at a nunnery are harbingers of merriment—or murder . . .

"A good mystery . . . excellently drawn . . . very authentic . . . the essence of a truly historical story is that the people should feel and believe according to their times. Margaret Frazer has accomplished this extraordinarily well."
—Anne Perry

THE OUTLAW'S TALE

Sister Frevisse meets a long-lost blood relative—but the blood may be on his hands . . .

*DON'T MISS THESE COMPELLING
NOVELS OF MEDIEVAL MYSTERY
AVAILABLE FROM BERKLEY PRIME CRIME!*

MORE MYSTERIES FROM THE
BERKLEY PUBLISHING GROUP . . .

SISTER FREVISSE MYSTERIES: Medieval mystery in the tradition of Ellis Peters . . .

by Margaret Frazer
THE NOVICE'S TALE   THE SERVANT'S TALE
THE OUTLAW'S TALE   THE BISHOP'S TALE

RENAISSANCE MYSTERIES: Sigismondo the sleuth courts danger — and sheds light on
the darkest of deeds . . .   "Most entertaining!"   —*Chicago Tribune*

by Elizabeth Eyre
DEATH OF THE DUCHESS   CURTAINS FOR THE CARDINAL

PENNYFOOT HOTEL MYSTERIES: In Edwardian England, death takes a seaside
holiday . . .

by Kate Kingsbury
ROOM WITH A CLUE   DO NOT DISTURB
SERVICE FOR TWO   EAT, DRINK, AND BE BURIED

THE BISHOP'S TALE

MARGARET FRAZER

BERKLEY PRIME CRIME, NEW YORK

THE BISHOP'S TALE

A Berkley Prime Crime Book / published by arrangement with the author

PRINTING HISTORY
Berkley Prime Crime edition / December 1994

ISBN: 0-425-14492-5

Berkley Prime Crime Books are published by
The Berkley Publishing Group,
200 Madison Avenue, New York, NY 10016.
The name BERKLEY PRIME CRIME and the BERKLEY PRIME CRIME
design are trademarks belonging to Berkley Publishing Corporation.

PRINTED IN THE UNITED STATES OF AMERICA

10 9 8 7 6 5 4 3 2 1

And whan that this was doon, thus spak that oon:
"Now lat us sitte and drynke, and make us merie,
And afterward we wol his body berie."

The Pardoner's Tale
Geoffrey Chaucer

Chapter

1

THE ROOM WAS in darkness except for the candles burning at the head of the bed and a gray line of thin daylight along the edge of the closely shuttered windows. The coals in the brazier in the corner had burned too low even to glow, though the room was still thickly warm with their heat and the crowding of people who had been there.

Now there were only two men, and one of them was dying.

Thomas Chaucer lay motionless in the wide bed, raised a little on his pillows. It was a rich bed, with the glint of gold threads in the embroidered coverlet and hung with pattern-woven curtains. And what could be seen of the room in the small reach of the candlelight was equally rich, the furnishings deeply carved, the ceiling beams painted in twined vines and singing birds. Now, for this occasion, one of the chests along the wall was covered with a white cloth and set out for priestly matters. Between two stately burning beeswax candles were a small vessel of sacred oil, another of holy water, and a golden box for the consecrated wafers. Cardinal Bishop Beaufort of Winchester, tall beyond the ordinary and seeming more so in his furred, scarlet gown and in the low light, moved from the chest to stand beside the bed again. His voice moved richly, surely, through the Latin words.

"*Accipe, frater, Viaticum Corporis Domini nostri Jesu Christi, qui te custodiat ab hoste maligno, et perducat in vitam aeternam, amen.*" Accept, brother, the Body of our Lord Jesus Christ, who keep you from the evil host, and lead you into eternal life, amen.

With great care and gentleness, the bishop laid the fragment of Christ's body on Chaucer's tongue. Weakly, he swallowed it, then whispered, "My last food. And the best."

"To nourish your soul rather than your body," Beaufort agreed. He moved away, his back to the bed and the dying man.

"Hal," Chaucer said.

Not turning around, Beaufort said huskily, "Yes?"

"Stay with me this while. It won't be much longer."

Still with his back to the bed, Beaufort bent his head, wiped his eyes, then straightened and turned. "You are probably the last person who will ever call me Hal," he said, his lightness strained over grief. "The last who remembers when we were young."

"Bedford may."

"Bedford is in France and sick with what's been done to him. I doubt he'll ever see England again."

Chaucer took that in silence awhile. "Then consider the benefits of there being no one left to remember your disreputable youth and tell stories on you."

Beaufort gave him the smile he wanted and laid a hand over his cold, thin arm. "I've learned to live with your exaggerated memories of my disreputable youth. But you'd best guard your tongue and thoughts lest I have to absolve you all over again." Belatedly, he removed the purple stole from around his neck, kissed it, folded it, and set it aside.

Beaufort and Chaucer were cousins. Their mothers had been sisters, the daughters of a Flemish knight in the queen's retinue five kings ago. Chaucer's mother had suitably married an officer of the royal duke of Lancaster's household named Geoffrey Chaucer. From their solid and respectable marriage, by his father's connections and his own considerable talents, Thomas had built a fortune and his life.

Beaufort's mother had been less conventional. She had borne the royal duke of Lancaster four children without benefit of marriage. But years later, to everyone's surprise and for no reason except love, the duke had actually married her. Their children had been legitimized under the name of Beaufort, and Henry—sometimes Hal—their second son, had risen high in both the Church and England's government. And built a fortune so great he was chief lender to the Crown in its necessity.

Despite the differences between them, they had been and were good friends, with deep respect for the men they each had become. The silence between them now was companionable under its weight of grief.

A candle hissed over a flaw in its wick, and Beaufort said, "You don't want Matilda to come in again? Or Alice?"

Chaucer's wife and daughter had left the room during the last rites, taking the servants and attendants and Matilda's contained but continuous weeping with them. If any returned, all returned, and the room would be crowded and intense with them again. Eyes closed, Chaucer said with the barest movement of his lips, "No." And then, after another silence, he said, "There's something I want you to do for me."

"Anything in my power." Which was considerable.

"In the aumbry, there . . ." Chaucer moved his head slightly to show which cupboard along the wall he meant. "There's a book. Wrapped in cloth. It's not in my will, but give it to my niece. The nun. Dame Frevisse." A smile turned the corners of his mouth. "But don't you look at it. Leave it wrapped."

"Secret books to young women, Thomas?" Beaufort teased mildly. "Am I supposed to approve?"

"You'd have to officially disapprove if you knew what it was, but I believe I imperil neither her soul nor my own with it." He added irrelevantly, "Nor is she so young anymore."

"I suppose she isn't, is she? She's been in her nunnery quite a while." Beaufort looked in the aumbry for the book and found it. It was small, hardly as long as his hand, but bulky, even allowing for its wrappings. He ran his fingers along the edges he could feel through the cloth. "Not something I'd want for my own library, I trust?"

Chaucer smiled a little more. "All the best of my books are already safely named to you in my will. No, this is a plain thing that Frevisse valued in the while she lived here. I like to think of her having it."

"Then she will." Beaufort laid the book on the white-clothed chest and returned to Chaucer's side. "By the way, won't your son-in-law protest the gutting of your library on my behalf?"

"My son-in-law judges a book by how many jewels are set in its cover and how bright with gold the pictures are. I've left the gaudiest for him. He'll be content."

"He'd best be," Beaufort said. "I doubt he'd care to deal with me over the matter." Chaucer's daughter had married William de la Pole, Earl of Suffolk, for her third husband. He had a great inherited fortune, a handsome face, a remarkable degree of charm, influence in the government, and—in Chaucer's and Beaufort's opinions—not much in the way of brains, and even less in the way of common sense. There was no doubt that Suffolk would come off the worse if it came to a dispute, for Beaufort was a match for anyone in the kingdom.

No, it had not been lack of ability that had kept Beaufort from rising to the highest place in the royal government—Protector to the young King Henry VI—but a regrettable clash of character between himself and his own half-nephew on his father's side. If plain hatred—God forgive him for it—could have killed, Humphrey, duke of Gloucester, would have long since been quite dead. As it was, they had succeeded in crabbing each other's ambitions; though each had high power and place, neither of them had as much as they wanted, and neither had gained control of the young King's government. Nor were they likely to, now that he was nearing an age to take more responsibility to himself. Unless one could keep near enough to him to win his favor and support. . .

Beaufort realized he had lost himself in his thoughts. And that Chaucer was watching him with familiar mockery, or the faint shadow of it that was all he had strength for.

"All right," Beaufort said. "I was 'indulging in my ambitions,' as you have been wont to say. Will it be a comfort to you if I admit I've begun to think you were right to refuse so steadily to be drawn into the morass I've willingly braved all these years?"

Chaucer moved his head in weak denial. "No. I've always known I was right to avoid Westminster like the plague. Though, like the plague, it cannot always be avoided." With a smile, he added, "But I've also known you were where you belonged, Hal, given your very different ambitions from mine. I'd be sorry to hear you've wearied of it?"

Tentatively—and Chaucer was probably the only man in England to whom he would show that side of himself—Beaufort said, "The King is growing older. Things are changing."

"To your advantage perhaps."

"Perhaps," Beaufort assented. If Bedford died in France—the man who had both supported him and curbed him, keeping a balance among the court factions no matter how they resented it—then there would be new possibilities.

Chaucer's eyes closed, not in sleep, Beaufort thought, but simply because he lacked strength to hold them open. The pulse in his throat fluttered and lost beat. Beaufort leaned forward, a sick feeling in his own heart. But the pulse steadied, weakly, into a slow rhythm again and went on. Chaucer had been dying for three months now, had known for certain he was dying, though the wasting disease itself had begun to come on him a while before that. Nothing he ate gave him any strength; despite everything done for him—and he could afford the best physicians in England—he had wasted as simply as if he had been deliberately starving. Now there was very little of him left; his failing body could not hold on to his spirit much longer.

Without opening his eyes, Chaucer said, "Lydgate."

Beaufort almost looked around the room to see who had come in.

"If he sends a poem about me," Chaucer said, his eyes still closed, "I strictly charge you that it isn't to be read at my funeral or at any of my memorials. Not a word, not a line of it."

"But . . ." Lydgate was England's master poet, brilliant, popular, prolific. He wrote on every great occasion, at length. His many-versed cry of pain at Chaucer's departure for a stay in France won high praise. And he claimed Thomas's own father Geoffrey as his inspiration. So it was perhaps surprising that Thomas had always been, privately but unremittingly, rude about his work.

"Unless you are quite sure I won't come to haunt you in some particularly horrible guise, don't let any of his work be read anywhere near me, dead or alive. Not at my funeral, my month's mind, my year day, or any other time."

Beaufort twitched his lips tightly over a smile he could not help, while allowing the tears to flow. Customary as tears might be among the gently born, yet he had not cried as wholeheartedly for anyone since his mother died, far more than thirty years ago. It was a minute or two before he could say, "You have my word you'll be spared him, even in death."

Chaucer's eyebrows lifted, but his eyes did not open. He took a shallow breath, and another, and said more faintly, "My niece. The nun. I've told you about her?"

"You've told me. I have the book. I'll give it to her."

"Tell her . . . I'll miss her."

Chapter

◙ 2 ◙

FREVISSE BENT LOWER and rested her forehead on the cold stone of the altar step, her clasped hands pressed against her breast, her knees aching beneath her. She had been there since the end of Tierce, the mid-morning office. Soon it would be Sext, and the other nuns of St. Frideswide's Priory would be returning. She would have to rise and take her place with them in the choir, and she was not certain her knees would hold her when the time came to stand.

She sighed and straightened, raising her eyes to the lamp burning above the altar. Its oil was renewed by caring hands every day, its small flame deeply cupped in the curve of red glass. It burned without wavering, simple and enduring among the shadows and cold air eddies of the church, and life.

Frevisse shivered. She was lately caught in a cold eddy of life and could not seem to escape it, despite all her prayers and penance. Half a year ago she had made choices and a final choice that had come because of them—and since then had lived with what she had done, and found no peace. There were people dead who might have been alive except

9

for her choices. *Mea culpa, mea culpa, mea maxima culpa.*
By my fault, by my fault, by my most grievous fault.

As if in sympathy with her sorrow, the days had been
gray and damp and chill under lowering skies for seemingly
as long as she could remember. It had been summer, a long
time ago, but there had been few warm days among the chill
and wet. Then had come the rainy autumn, and what there
had been of harvest had rotted in the fields. Now, hardly
passed Martinmas, late November in the year of God's grace
1434, there was nothing to look forward to but a famine
winter and much dying, as if the world were a reflection of
her soul.

Frevisse's mouth drew down tightly at the thought. That
was her self speaking, the worldly self she had been so
harshly purging all these months.

The prioress had understood her sickness of heart. In the
shifting of duties she had made at Midsummer, Domina
Edith had ruled that Frevisse would cease to be hosteler,
seeing to the priory's guests and always in contact with
matters outside the cloister. Instead, she was made novice
mistress, her duties to oversee such novices as the priory
had—which was presently none, and none expected. In
place of them, she was set to copying in her fine hand any
books the prioress had promised to someone or had borrowed for the priory—which in the months since Midsummer had been one.

Frevisse had been grateful for this lessening of outward
responsibility, had understood that Domina Edith had given
it to her so she would have the chance to mend her sins and
inward hurt. And she had tried. But there was still no joy or
even simple pleasure in anything she did or prayed. And that
was another sin, the deadly one of accidie. God forgave all

sins repented of, but one's heart had to be open to receive the forgiveness.

The cloister bell began to clang flatly, telling it was time for Sext. Wearily, Frevisse crossed herself and rose painfully to her feet. The offices, seven times each day, from midnight through to bed again, were her comfort and refuge. She almost always could forget herself in their complex beauties of interwoven psalms and prayers, and find a momentary promise that this dryness of her heart and spirit would not last forever.

But it was not ended yet. Weary of herself, she went the little way beyond the altar to her place in the choir, knelt there and waited, her head bowed.

Quietly in their soft-soled shoes, with only a rustle of skirts, the other nuns came from whatever tasks they had been doing throughout the priory. St. Frideswide's was a small Benedictine house; there were only ten nuns and their prioress. Frevisse could identify them all by their footfalls. Sister Thomasine first, her light, hurried steps reflecting her eagerness. To serve as a nun had been her only desire since girlhood, and, still hardly more than a girl, she cherished it with her whole heart. It had been a shock to her when Domina Edith had appointed her infirmaress in place of Dame Claire. And a shock to Dame Claire, who had been taken from her beloved herbs and potions and tending to the sick to become cellarer and kitchener, supervising the priory's lay workers, storerooms, and kitchen. Dame Claire's firm, even footsteps followed Sister Thomasine's, with a mingling of two others close behind her—Sisters Emma and Juliana, neither hurried nor lagging, simply tending to another of the tasks of a nun. Behind them, with no mistaking her heavy tread, came Dame Alys. She had taken her loss of authority as cellarer with ill grace, and made a discontented sacrist. After her, by a goodly while, rushed Sister Amicia, nearly late as usual.

Domina Edith did not enter until Sister Amicia was in her place. The prioress's dignity required she not be part of the crush and bustle of her nuns. But she was only waiting, and entered as soon as Sister Amicia had settled breathlessly into her stall. Dame Perpetua and Sister Lucy were on her either side, hands on her elbows to steady and support her as she shuffled to her place in her own elaborately carved choir stall. Domina Edith was very old, and last winter's deep cold had dealt harshly with her. She had survived a heavy rheum in her chest but not recovered her strength. Frevisse, risen to her feet with the others, watched her slow coming and painful easing down into her seat with concern. Domina Edith had been prioress since the year Henry of Lancaster had made himself King Henry IV; Frevisse could not and did not want to imagine St. Frideswide's without her.

The prioress had just been settled in her stall when the bell in the church tower began to ring the hour of Sext.

Sext was a brief service. Frevisse refuged in it as deeply as she could for its little while, and at its end prayed with especial longing, *"Domine, exaudi orationem meum, et clamor meus ad te veniat."* Lord, hear my prayer, and let my cry come to you.

The prayer faded to the church's silence. For a moment there was no stir or whisper, only a silence heavy with the holy weight of the many prayers offered in this place.

Then Domina Edith leaned forward, and Dame Perpetua and Sister Lucy came quickly to help her to her feet. The others rose respectfully, holding their places until she was gone before going their own ways, brisk now to be about their other duties. As they left, Frevisse slid forward onto her kneeler again, returning to the words of Sext's opening hymn. *Rector potens, verax Deus . . . Confer salutem corporum veramque pacem cordium . . .* Lord of might, God of truth . . . Give the body health and true peace to the heart . . .

The health she asked for Domina Edith. Let her live, if it be your will. But for herself, peace to the heart, *pacem cordium,* peace . . .

A touch on her shoulder brought her back. A little dazed, Frevisse raised her head to find Dame Perpetua leaning over the choir stall in front of her to reach her.

It was difficult to judge each other's ages in St. Frideswide's, enveloped as they all were in the loose-fitted layers of the black Benedictine habit, only their faces showing in the surround of white wimples and black veils, with even then very little of their foreheads and nothing below the chin. But Frevisse guessed that Dame Perpetua was perhaps ten years older than herself, and so somewhere in her forties. She was a compactly built woman with a kind face and firm manner. Now, bound by the rule of silence, she smiled at Frevisse and made the hand gesture that meant the prioress, and another that asked Frevisse to come with her.

The prioress's parlor overlooked the inner yard and the guesthalls that flanked its gateway through three tall windows above a window seat made comfortable with brightly embroidered cushions. Because the prioress's duties included receiving the occasional important visitors and conducting business that could not be dealt with in the general chapter meetings, her quarters offered more comfort than the rest of the nunnery. There was a large, carved table covered by a woven Spanish tapestry, two chairs, and a fireplace, its flames crackling along a log to ward off the chill of this gray morning.

Domina Edith's own high-backed chair had been moved close to the hearth, and she sat there, wrapped in the fur-lined cloak she wore only upon the insistence of the infirmaress. It was drawn up to her chin and she was sunk down into it, smaller, it seemed to Frevisse, with each passing month. Just now, she might have been dozing, her chin deep into the folds of her wimple; but if she was, it was the light sleep of the aged. She lifted her head at Frevisse's entering, her faded eyes alert under the wrinkled lids.

"Dame Frevisse," she said, and Frevisse curtsied to her. "Sit." She gestured to the stool across the hearth from her.

Frevisse sat and was immediately aware of the fire's warmth on her cheeks. Her urge was to hold her hands out to it, too, but they were tucked decently up her sleeves, out of sight; it would be a luxury to bring them out.

"There is a letter come for you." Domina Edith nodded at Dame Perpetua, who had waited beside the table and now came forward with a folded, sealed piece of parchment in her hand.

Frevisse had supposed Domina Edith wished to see her about some failure in her duties or to warn her against so much time spent alone in the church. Changing her attention to the letter, she took it, not recognizing the handwriting on its outside that directed it to Dame Frevisse Barrett, St. Frideswide's Priory, near Banbury, Oxfordshire.

"I fear it is bad news," Domina Edith said softly.

As she said it, Frevisse turned the letter over and recognized her uncle Thomas Chaucer's seal imprint in the wax. But if it was his letter, then why had someone else written the address? That had never been his way before. Her hands beginning to tremble, because she knew he had been ill, Frevisse freed the seal and unfolded the letter, to find it was indeed written in her uncle's familiar hand.

"To my well-beloved niece, may this find you in health,
I greet you well, with God's blessing and mine. I am
dying—"

Frevisse drew her breath in sharply. All of her tightened
with pain, and she fought to keep herself steady. The letter
was brief and completely to the point, without any trace of
his usual dry wit.

"The disease that we hoped would draw off has indeed
proved fatal after all. I would see you one more time, if God
grants it and your good prioress allows your journey. . . ."
Frevisse's tears fell down onto the paper, blotting the ink.
With a harsh hand, she drove others from her eyes and read
on. "If not, know I hold you dear and will remember you in
heaven. Your uncle, Thomas Chaucer."

Already blind again with tears, Frevisse held the letter out
to Domina Edith, it being the prioress's right and duty—and
in this case, necessity—to read whatever came to her nuns.
She waited, hands pressed to her face to control her crying,
until Domina Edith said with all kindness, "You will leave
within the hour. May God bring you to him in time."

Chapter

3

THE COLD DAY was drawn down to a thin line of sullen red, lowering in the west below the roiling, darkening clouds. It was as much brightness as the day had seen, but the rain had held off, and the wind with its cutting edge was at their backs now as the four riders covered the last stretch of road, down into the valley with its village and the cluster of walls and buildings that was Ewelme Manor and the end of their journey.

They were already too late. They had learned in the last village before this that Chaucer had died. "Yesterday," a man had said. "Aye, yesterday. We heard the bell tolling. Carried on the wind, it was. And then today we heard for certain sure that it was over for him. God keep him."

So all their haste now was to escape the bitter cold and harsh wind; after two days of winter riding those were reasons enough. The small lake between the village and the manor house had a froth of whitecaps, and the tall elms around it soughed and bent their bare limbs in black, tossing patterns against the moving sky.

Ewelme's outer gates still stood open, with torches burning in the brackets to either side. As the riders came into the courtyard, grooms ran out from the stables, and there were hands to hold the horses and help the riders down.

Frevisse, dismounting stiff and clumsy with cold, looked among the grooms for a face she recognized. Ewelme was where she thought of when she thought of home; she had been part of her uncle's household for the eight final years of her girlhood.

But she had been gone too many years, it seemed. No one was familiar, including the short gentleman who, as the horses were led away, bobbed up under the travelers' noses, looking in each of their faces to determine who led their party. Even allowing for the layers of clothing and the cloak he was bundled in, he was a round-bodied man, and he bounced and jounced on the balls of his feet like a water-filled pig's bladder to show how eager he was to serve.

"Yes, yes, welcome! It's going to be a cruel night, indeed it is. So you're very welcome to shelter here. Of course you are. But you know, perhaps, we're a house bereaved. We can offer shelter, certainly, but—"

"I'm Master Chaucer's niece," Frevisse cut in curtly. "He sent for me. Before he died," she added, to be spared being told again that she was too late.

"Oh. Oh." The little man registered true distress. He was inches shorter than she was and cricked his neck sideways to see up to her face. "You heard on the way, then! How cruel, how distressing! My deepest sympathy!" He looked around at her companions. Dame Perpetua stood beside her; it was unthinkable a nun would travel without another nun for propriety's sake. And beyond them were the two burly men the priory steward had chosen from the priory's stables to accompany them. Given the times and season, any traveler with sense went well guarded if possible.

The little man seemed about to deal with one of the men, anticipating that the women might collapse into hysterical grief at any moment. But Frevisse was too tired and cold, and aware that Dame Perpetua was, as well, to waste time in displays of grief. Tersely, taking the situation in hand, she said, "Let my men be seen to in the stables, if that is convenient." The little man nodded, blinking rapidly at this display of authority. Frevisse did not give him a chance to speak his agreement, but turned to the priory men and directed, "Return to St. Frideswide's tomorrow. We'll be here for I don't know how long, but if it's to be more than a fortnight, we'll send word. When we're free to return, my aunt will arrange escort for us, surely."

She looked at the little man for confirmation. He bobbed his head emphatically. "Oh, surely, surely," he agreed.

"Then Dame Perpetua and I would be most grateful to go inside."

"Surely, surely."

As the two priory men bowed awkwardly and began to follow one of the grooms toward the stables, Dame Perpetua said, "God grant you a good night's rest."

Ashamed she had forgotten that simple courtesy, Frevisse added hastily, "And a safe journey home."

The men bowed again, in a hurry to be away to shelter and food. Frevisse and Dame Perpetua gave themselves over to the little man's guidance.

Ewelme was a moated manor house. As they crossed the bridge from the outer yard after the little man, the wind caught at them again, colder than before. But there were servants standing ready to hold the doors open, and on the little man's heels they came out of the wind and darkness

into a passage where elaborate wooden screens averted the
drafts that had come in with them. Beyond the passage was
the great hall that was the heart and gathering place of the
house. It was full of torchlight and the sounds of trestle
tables being set up. "Nearly supper time," the man explained, as if they would not know this. "Now . . ." He
hesitated. Apparently he had not decided what to do about
them in the time from the stable yard to here. Should it be
food and warmth first? Or ought they to be taken to Mistress
Chaucer right away? Or . . .

Frevisse thought he must be one of her aunt's choices for
office; her uncle had always expected quick-witted competence and dignity from those who directly served him.
Impatiently, and instantly displeased at herself for it, she
said, "I want to see my uncle. And Dame Perpetua wants a
warm fire to sit beside until it's time to eat. I'm sure Aunt
Matilda will want to know that we've arrived."

"Yes, yes, that seems the best way," the man agreed.
"Your uncle is in the chapel, my lady. If you'll come with
me . . ."

"I know the way. See to Dame Perpetua."

Dame Perpetua gave her a grateful, shivering smile and nod.
She was a good traveler, not given to complaint and grateful
for whatever comforts came her way, but she had reached the
end of her endurance and needed warmth and a place to sit.
She followed the little man away.

There was no warmth in the chapel, though the many
candles around the coffin gave the illusion of it. Frevisse
paused in the doorway, shivering, remembering when Aunt
Matilda had agitated for a fireplace in here. . . . "There,
along the outer wall. It would be no trouble at all to have it
built." But Chaucer had answered, "We come here for the
good of our souls, not the comforting of our bodies." And

though he had had no objection to comforting his body at another time and place with all the luxuries his considerable fortune could afford, he had held firm about the chapel. There was no fireplace, and chill seemed to breathe from its stones.

But he had been lavish in its decorations. The main worshipping for the household was done in the village church, where the funeral and burial would be held. The chapel was meant solely for private family devotions, and the household priest's daily mass, and was as gracefully complex and elegant as a saint's reliquary. The ceiling was painted heaven's blue and spangled with stars; the elaborately carved and gilded wood reredos behind the altar reached to them; and though now the altar was covered in black cloth rather than its usual embroidered richness, a long stretch of woven carpet in jewel-bright reds and blues and greens reached from it down the altar steps and the length of the chapel floor almost to the door. The side walls were painted with saints standing each by the other in a flowery mead, smiling benignly down on those who came to pray, while the rear wall was brilliant with the Virgin being crowned in heaven while saints and angels joyfully watched.

Seeing the Virgin, Frevisse could hear her uncle singing lightly, "Had the apple not been taken, taken been, Then would not Our Lady have been crowned heaven's queen, heaven's queen . . ." as he had done the day he had explained all the meanings in the picture to her, when she was small and newly come to Ewelme and still wary of its strangeness.

Now his coffin was set on trestles in front of the altar, with two priests and two servants of the household kneeling among the candles around it, their prayers a small, sibilant murmur in the quiet. Until he was buried, he would never be left unattended.

Frevisse went forward silently until she could see his face. The candlelight gave it a warmth it no longer truly had, and as was so usual with the peaceful dead, he looked to be only sleeping. But it would never again be any use for her to think, *Remember this, to tell him when he comes to visit next.* Or hope, in this world, to talk and argue with him, or hear his laughter.

Frevisse found the pain of her grief still too raw and unfamiliar to bear. She dropped her eyes, knelt where she was, and began her prayers for his soul's safety and rest. She had prayed so much these past months, against her thick misery of doubts and a different kind of grief, that the prayers came with instinctive ease and no need to grope for words.

Lost in her prayers and grief, she was unaware of any movement around her until a hand briefly touched her shoulder and someone said, "You had best come to supper now. Your aunt will want to see you as soon as may be."

She became aware that the stone under the carpet was pressing hard on her knees, and that around her there was a shifting and murmur as those who had been praying gave over their places to those come to replace them. Her face was warm and wet with tears, and she had no idea how long she had been there. There was no hope of hiding that she had been crying, and she did not try as she lifted her head to the man standing beside her.

She recognized him as one of the priests who had been praying beside the coffin when she entered. He had the drawn look of someone who had been praying for an uncomfortably long while; but there was the sheen behind his weariness that told how rich his praying had been.

She let him take her elbow and help her rise, not questioning how he knew who she was. Chaucer's niece, the nun, had been expected. And she *was* hungry. Broken out of her prayers, she was suddenly aware of all her body's discomforts, with hunger for food and warmth very strong among them.

"Thank you," she said. With her hands tucked into her sleeves and her head down, she followed him not back to the great hall where most of the household would dine, but aside and up the stairs to her aunt's parlor.

Frevisse had spent countless uncomfortable hours there in her girlhood, learning and working the intricate, eternal embroideries and stitchery considered a suitable occupation for a lady, and listening to her aunt talk. Aunt Matilda always talked, to Frevisse, to her women, sometimes to the empty air. Aunt Matilda was fond of talk, and that had been the original reason Frevisse had sought the refuge of her uncle's relatively quiet company, among his work and books. Later, love of what those books held had been the stronger motive. Her uncle had been far better company than her aunt; he listened as much as he talked, and his mind ranged through all the learning and lessons he had gathered into his library and his life. Aunt Matilda had thought Frevisse's choice very unladylike, of course, but since dear Thomas allowed it, she had been willing to let it be.

Aside from her boredom, Frevisse remembered her aunt's parlor as a lovely room, well-proportioned and high-ceilinged, with ample windows to fill it with light even on cloudy days. It looked out on the moat with its swans and, in summer, the green reaches of the park. With her own inherited wealth and her husband's constantly growing fortune, Aunt Matilda had furnished it with every comfort. And though tonight the shutters were closed across the

windows, top and bottom, shadows were banished to the
lowest, farthest corners by lamps burning on every flat
surface, all around the room. Their rich, steady light
gleamed on the painted patterns of the shutters and ceiling
beams, and caught among the bright threads of the wall-
hung tapestries. Braziers glowed in the corners, warming
the room, and it was so crowded with people that in the first
moments of her arrival, Frevisse failed to recognize anyone.

Then she saw her aunt. Richly gowned and veiled in
black, she was seated at the room's far end, in front of the
brightest tapestry. On her right, in another chair, sat a
younger woman in equally rich black whom Frevisse
guessed was her daughter Alice, so that the man seated
beyond her was undoubtedly Alice's latest husband, William de la Pole, the earl of Suffolk.

The identity of the man seated to Aunt Matilda's left was
more problematical. For a moment, unable to have clear
view of him among the crowded shift of people in the room,
Frevisse could not even guess who he might be. But then
she saw him clearly. A churchman by the severe cut of his
floor-length black gown and the priest's cap he wore to
cover his tonsure. But even the length of the room away, she
knew he was anything but a plain churchman; he held
himself like a prince, and quite abruptly she realized who he
was, though she had seen him no more than twice in her
girlhood. Cardinal Bishop Beaufort of Winchester. A prince
of the Church indeed, and doing the family great honor by
his presence.

Then Aunt Matilda, whose eye was ever as busy as her
tongue, saw her, broke off whatever condolences she had
been receiving, and, rising from her chair with an exclamation, surged toward her, arms extended. "Frevisse, my dear!
My precious dear!" She was a tall woman, comfortably

plump in her middle age. Her black veiling, enough for half a dozen women, drifted and fell about them both as she wrapped her arms around Frevisse and held her close. "I knew you would be too late; he went so suddenly at the end, almost as soon as the letter was sent. I don't know what I shall do without him, what any of us shall do without him. But you're here. Bless you, my dear."

Enveloped in her aunt's embrace and overflow of words, Frevisse murmured only, "Dear aunt," which seemed to be sufficient.

But then there was the necessity of being introduced, first to the room at large: "My very dear niece, Dame Frevisse of St. Frideswide's Priory. Dear Thomas was so fond of her, and she's come too late to bid him farewell, but she's here to my comfort, and I'm so glad." Then to the three people still seated in front of the tapestry on the room's only chairs: "My lord of Winchester, may I present my dear niece Dame Frevisse." Aunt Matilda drew Frevisse directly in front of him. "Frevisse, this is the Cardinal Bishop Henry Beaufort. He came all the way from Westminster—imagine that—to be with Thomas at the end. He and Thomas are cousins. You remember him, surely."

Frevisse sank in a deep curtsy. "My lord bishop," she said, and took the hand he held out to her, to kiss the proper ring among the many that he wore. All of them were ornate, most set with red stones shaded from ruby to garnet. To go with his cardinal's robes, she supposed, noting that his gown was of the richest wool and lined with black fur. The jewels and sable showed he was undoubtedly as wealthy as rumor said. And that was only one of the many things rumor said about him.

But apart from what little Chaucer had said of him to her, rumor was all she knew about him. She was disconcerted, as she straightened and met his gaze, to find him regarding her with a speculative assessment deeper than the commonplace nature of their meeting.

But all he said, in most formal wise, was, "Your loss is as mine in this."

So it was sufficient for her to answer, with an acknowledging bow of her head, "A great loss and a deep grief to us both." Then she was free to move away from him to meet her cousin Alice.

She had seen her uncle fairly often and her aunt occasionally since she had entered St. Frideswide's. But she had last seen Alice seventeen years ago, when Alice had been thirteen and already two years widowed from her first husband. Since then, she had grown into womanhood, married the earl of Salisbury, been widowed again by his death at the siege of Orleans, and a few years ago married the earl of Suffolk.

When Frevisse had known her, she had been a quiet, mannered child, neither unsatisfactorily plain nor noticeably lovely, and much better at her sewing than Frevisse had ever hoped to be. Remembering her then, Frevisse was disconcerted now to be confronted by a woman as tall as herself and quite lovely, her blue eyes perfect almond shapes and brilliant with warmth and intelligence as she rose from her chair and took Frevisse's hand. "It's been a long while, cousin, and now a sad occasion to meet again," she said, her voice as gracious as her movements.

Frevisse murmured a reply, trying to reconcile her memories of her little cousin to this poised, grown woman. She was not perfectly beautiful; her face and nose and upper lip were all somewhat long, but they were in proportion with each other, and to judge by her eyebrows and rose-sweet complexion, she was still pale-fair. It was not difficult to see how she had married twice into the high nobility, even putting her father's wealth aside.

Alice's husband, William, the earl of Suffolk, had also risen to be introduced. He was taller than Alice, his brown hair attractively graying at the temples, his demeanor suitably grave. But he had a merry mouth, given to laughter at other times, Frevisse supposed. He was handsome in the expected ways—his strong features even, his jaw firm, his brow broad, his nose well-shaped. He made a striking mate to Alice; their children should be good to look on. But he patted Frevisse's hand with condescending comfort after he had bowed to kiss it, and as he spoke a few sentences perfectly suited to the occasion, he was more aware of how well he said them than whether they were a comfort to her. Frevisse decided she would avoid him as much as possible.

The arrival of servants with supper freed Frevisse from receiving other condolences. Alice and Suffolk and most of the others were going down to dine in the hall with the household, but Aunt Matilda was to dine in the parlor with Bishop Beaufort. "And I'd have you dine here, too, my dear. With your—Dame Perpetua? You're both exhausted, I'm sure, and this will be so much easier than the hall."

Frevisse readily agreed. As the small table was set up, she went aside to where Dame Perpetua had fallen into quiet conversation with the priest who had brought Frevisse from the chapel. He was apparently staying to dine, too, and acknowledged her approach with a slight inclination of his head.

Dame Perpetua made the introductions. "This is Sir Philip. He's been priest here—" She looked at him questioningly. "Three years now?"

"Come Advent," he agreed.

Frevisse bowed her head slightly in return. "Sir Philip."

"Dame Frevisse."

His voice was pleasant, even and well-modulated, matching the good bones of a face that would have been handsome except for the deep pitting and white webbing of smallpox scars from chin to cheeks to temples. His black hair was a smooth cap clipped fashionably short above the ears, and his black priest's gown, like the bishop's, was of rich wool despite its conservative cut. Unlike the bishop, he wore no jewels except a single, deeply etched gold ring, but it was plain he was no poor priest eking out a living on the margins of the Church; his manners were as smooth as any courtier's. The three of them made polite talk concerning the weather and the discomforts of travel until they were called to the table.

Conversation at the meal was strange in its normalcy, as if they had come together for the pleasure of each other's company. It began predictably with Aunt Matilda's comments on the bad weather. She was kind to include Dame Perpetua in her questions and comments, and Dame Perpetua was careful never to presume too much familiarity in her answers. She had been brought up in a home much like this, had learned to be both gentle and detailed in her manners. That was one of the reasons Domina Edith had chosen her for Dame Frevisse's companion. "She will not add to your troubles, nor disgrace the nunnery with forward ways," the prioress had said.

Indeed, Dame Perpetua replied quietly and gracefully to anything said to her, and when the conversation went away from her, she let it go. She might have been totally unaware of the importance of Bishop Beaufort seated imposingly to her right at one end of the table, so perfect was her demeanor.

For Frevisse it was less easy to be so gracious. Her aunt's

bright, familiar chatter was strained over a real and lacerating grief. And beyond that, Frevisse was uncomfortably aware that Bishop Beaufort was still watching her beyond the social needs of the moment. Frevisse did not want his interest. She wanted the evening to be over and to be alone in bed with her thoughts and grieving until tomorrow had to be faced. But first there was this supper to be endured, and now, amid the talk of the poor harvest, he asked her directly, "How are matters at your nunnery? Were you able to save any of the harvest?"

Careful to keep her voice neutral, revealing nothing but information and politeness, Frevisse answered, "Perhaps enough to see us through until next year if we're very spare with it." She should have stopped there, but honesty made her add, "And perhaps not if we need to give to the villagers, as we did last year." Then, betrayed by the need to know, she asked, "Will there be any wheat brought in from abroad? How were the French harvests?"

"France went much the way we did, except in the extreme south, which is of no use to us," Bishop Beaufort answered readily. Below the Loire was French-held territory, where English rule did not run. "There is some dealing with the Hanse at present to bring wheat in from the Baltic east where the harvests have been good, we hear."

In the urgency of the matter—life or death for those who lacked money to buy wheat at prices inflated by the scarcity—Frevisse forgot her resolve to speak sparingly. If anyone present knew these things, it would be Bishop Beaufort. Leaning toward him, she asked, "And in the meantime will there be efforts to hold prices down here in England?"

The bishop paused in spooning up his next mouthful.

"Word has gone out from the Council to every town to do as much as they can toward that end."

That was a politician's answer. Frevisse's politeness slipped a little. She demanded rather than asked, "How much toward that end do you think they'll do?"

"Frevisse, dear, have you tried one of these cakes?" Aunt Matilda gestured for a servant to hold out to her a plate with small white cakes studded with raisins.

Frevisse began to shake her head, recognizing the tactic her aunt had employed frequently whenever Frevisse and Chaucer would fall into one of their cheerful, complex arguments over some matter Aunt Matilda had thought unseemly for the occasion. With abrupt meekness, and anger at herself for being more bold than she should have, Frevisse said, "Thank you, aunt," and turned her attention to one of the cakes. The conversation shifted to the question of how many and who would come to the funeral, set for the day after tomorrow.

But when she glanced up once toward Bishop Beaufort a while later, he was gazing at her with even more of an assessing look than he had had before.

Chapter
◼ 4 ◼

Aunt Matilda rose the next morning still gray with grief, and Alice, who had shared her mother's bed, showed her own weariness around her eyes. Frevisse and Dame Perpetua, with their hurried journey's ache and weariness still in them, had slept on the servants' truckle beds, while the servants and Alice's lady-in-waiting slept on straw-filled mattresses, all now pushed out of the way and out of sight under the tall bed.

For the two nuns, the morning preparations were simple: they were washed and dressed and their wimples and veils neatly pinned in place while Alice's lady-in-waiting was still combing out and braiding her lady's hair before dressing her. With hardly three words said between them, they drew aside to stand out of the way.

Frevisse, watching the bustle and chatter around her cousin and unnaturally silent aunt, remembered Chaucer once saying that men who are tired grow quiet, while women grow talkative. Aunt Matilda had clearly passed weariness to the edge of exhaustion. While laying out her lady's black gown for the day, Aunt Matilda's woman, Joan, in a tone only a servant of long standing would dare to use, said abruptly, "You've no business being out and about today, my lady. No one expects it of you. There's people enough to see to what needs doing."

"But the guests. Thomas would want—"

Alice cut in with, "Father would want you not to make yourself more ill than you already are."

She looked to Frevisse over Matilda's head, and Frevisse immediately said, "Truly, Aunt, you've been through weeks of enduring. Today will be full of people arriving for the funeral, and everyone wanting things from you if they see you, when what you need just now is to gather your strength for tomorrow. There's nothing today that Alice and I can't oversee or come to you when we need direction. Please, Aunt, listen to us on this."

Matilda shook her head refusingly through all of Frevisse's words. But at the end of them, Alice knelt before her, took her hands, and pleaded very sweetly, "Please, Mother. Let us do this for you."

Matilda closed her eyes over sudden tears. Her body slackened its rigid determination to go on, and in a faltering voice she said, "Perhaps, perhaps you're right. It's tomorrow I should be thinking of, when we . . . when we . . ." She could not say, "bury Thomas," but when, with visible effort, she had regained control, she opened her eyes and began to tell them everything that needed doing today.

Check the linen closet for blankets and set the stable hands to filling pallets with straw, she told them, then make sure the preparations for the funeral feast are under way and nothing is lacking in the kitchen, find sweet herbs to strew on the church floor, note every guest's rank on arrival—be there yourself to greet them, of course—and make sure they are in correct order for the procession to the church tomorrow and at the feast, see to it there is plenty of clean water so guests can wash up on arrival, don't let anyone mistake a washup bucket for a chamber pot, ensure families who are feuding with one another sleep far apart tonight and are not seated next to one another tomorrow, keep a fire burning in the great hall all day so arriving guests may warm themselves . . .

Alice and Frevisse shared a small grimace of mutual sympathy over Matilda's head as Joan encouraged her back into bed and the endless list faded to a weary murmur.

By early afternoon the influx of guests had become heavy. Nearest neighbors would come and go on the day itself, but the November days were short and anyone more than a few hours' ride away would come today and stay over at least two nights. Thomas Chaucer's connections had ranged from the ranks of merchants in London to the innermost circles of court power, with all of them important, but precedence had to be noted and scrupulously given. To her relief, Frevisse found that receiving the highest ranking among them fell naturally to her cousin Alice. As widow of the earl of Salisbury, and now wife of the earl of Suffolk, as well as daughter of the house, Alice was already acquainted with most of them; gracious in her duties, she reminded Frevisse both of the self-possessed little cousin Frevisse had last known, and of Chaucer himself.

Frevisse was left to see to the lesser folk, though lesser was a relative term. Landed knights and merchants wealthier than earls were hardly lesser. But it meant that she was waiting in the great hall when Sir Walter Fenner, head of the prominent and numerous Fenner family, was ushered in.

The Fenners were among the more prominent patrons of St. Frideswide's, though less generously and intrusively than they had been a few years ago, so Sir Walter and

Frevisse were already acquainted. Seeing him ushered into the hall, she had time to put on a polite face of mild pleasure tempered by the formal grief of the occasion, and said graciously, "How good that you could come, Sir Walter."

"My deep sorrow that it's for such a sad occasion, Dame," he replied. The Fenners had a long memory for offenses, and the last time they had met, he had accused her of hiding his mother's murderer. But he knew the needs of this moment; his politeness was brief but correct. "Your uncle's loss must grieve you deeply."

"Indeed it does, sir."

That was sufficient for both of them; but as he turned aside to follow the servant who would show him in, she saw that the squire with him was young Robert Fenner, who had aided her against Sir Walter's anger at St. Frideswide's that same time ago. In the three years since she had last seen him, he had left the last of boyhood for young manhood, Frevisse observed. But the brief, warm smile he cast her as he followed Sir Walter showed he remembered her.

Then the little, bouncing man—whom she had learned was Gallard Basing, the usher here—advanced on her with another newly arrived guest. "Sir Clement Sharpe," Gallard announced with unusual terseness, and stood aside.

Sir Clement was a lean, pallid man with thinning hair the dull brown of dead leaves, and eyes that matched it. He was elegantly dressed in a wide-cut dark blue houppelande amply trimmed with gray fur, and a long-liripiped hat that he had already removed for his bow to her, a bow a little more deep and flourished than need be.

"My lady, my profound regrets for your uncle's death."

"Thank you. We greatly appreciate your coming. Aunt Matilda will be pleased."

She did not understand the twitch of his mouth, or his

answer. "Assure her we'd settled the matter before he fell finally ill, and I'll not take any advantage over it."

She smiled and said, "I'm sure you won't." Because whatever the matter had been, it would not be Aunt Matilda he dealt with, but the earl of Suffolk's lawyers, for Suffolk and Alice were Chaucer's heirs.

"May I introduce my ward?" Sir Clement asked, and put back his hand to draw a girl forward. At first Frevisse thought she was a child, but a more careful look revealed she was more likely sixteen or seventeen, only small for her years and daintily built. "Lady Anne Featherstone."

Lady Anne curtsied. She was dressed in plain dark wool for travel, but her manners were as pretty as her face. Frevisse curtsied back but Sir Clement was already adding, less graciously, "And my nephew, Guy Sharpe."

There was little family resemblance between lean and pallid Sir Clement and the broad-chested, handsome young man who stepped forward on Lady Anne's other side. He bowed and said appropriate words of greeting, but rather than his words, Frevisse noted the warm, sideways look of affection that Lady Anne gave him as he did.

Frevisse was not sure if Sir Clement saw it, too, but before Guy had finished straightening, Sir Clement had begun to move away, drawing Lady Anne with him and to his other side, away from Guy, in one neat gesture. Frevisse saw the young man's face tighten, his eyes on Lady Anne even as he finished speaking to her, before he followed in Sir Clement's wake.

Frevisse hoped they kept in abeyance whatever coil of trouble they were building until they had left Ewelme.

A gap in travelers came late in the afternoon, and Frevisse left her duties to go to the chapel. Except for a brief time this morning, she had not been there since yesterday about this hour.

Neither the shadows nor the candlelight nor the cold had changed since then. Nor her grief. And she was still tired, though now from dealing with too many people and talking more than she was used to, rather than from cold and travel. Even the watchers around the coffin might have been the same as yesterday's; and then she saw that at least one of them was: the household priest, Sir Philip.

She stood awhile inside the doorway, letting the silence envelop and soothe her, before she finally knelt to pray. But she had barely begun when low voices outside the chapel's shut door broke her concentration. She tried to pray in spite of them, but although their words were obscured by the chapel door, their emotions were not. A young man and a woman—or perhaps a girl—her tone desperate, urging something to the man, who answered with an urgency of his own.

Then there was a third voice, another man's, raised loud enough to leave no doubt about what he said in anger and bitter satisfaction. "I *thought* you'd both disappeared most conveniently!"

The girl answered, her own words clear with matching anger now. "How did you know where we were? Who told you?"

"I'm not the fool you wish I were. There aren't that many places in a house this size and full of people you could go to be alone. Once Jevan said you were both gone, I could guess where you were easily enough."

"Jevan!" the girl said bitterly.

The young man began to say something, but was cut off scornfully by the older man answering, "You're just idiot enough to think that, boy!"

Goaded into raising his voice, the young man snapped, "Not so much an idiot as to think you can keep us apart forever!"

"You'd better think it, boy, because I can!"

The girl cried out desperately, "We love each other!"

Brushing past Frevisse on his way to the door, Sir Philip said under his breath, "Jesus, God in heaven."

Supposing the young woman might take better to her presence and hoping the men might abate their anger because of it, Frevisse rose to follow the priest.

In the small antechamber to the chapel, Sir Clement Sharpe had his nephew, Guy, and his ward, Lady Anne, blocked into a corner. Neither of the young couple looked intimidated or shamed; side by side, they faced his towering anger at them with anger of their own, the girl's hand laid possessively on Guy's arm.

She was dressed now in a dark amber, high-belted houppeland and had loosed her pale, honey-colored hair in a haze around her head and shoulders. In the shadowed room she looked as delicately lovely as a carven angel, her brightness the focus of the dark anger between the two men.

"Love has nothing to do with whom you marry," Sir Clement was saying with a sneer. "You marry whom you're told and to the best profit. I paid money for that right and profit, and you'll remember it!"

Before either Guy or Lady Anne could reply, Sir Philip said, "You'll do better to remember where you are, and why, and lower your voices."

His own voice was low, at church level, with no temper in it, but it stopped them and brought Sir Clement around to face him, clearly willing to turn his anger that way. But then with what Frevisse could only read as a dawning delight, he exclaimed, "God's sweet breath, it's Philip Base-born! You're looking well above your place in the world!"

"And you're disgracing yours," Sir Philip replied evenly. "This is a house in mourning, and on the other side of this door is the cause of it. Take your family squabbling somewhere else. Or better, let it be until you leave Ewelme."

Sir Clement cast a scornful glance at his nephew and Lady Anne. "Better to tell them than me!" he retorted. "It's their disobedience, not—"

"You're too loud in the near presence of God and death," Sir Philip interposed.

"Don't you dare speak to me like that, you field whelp! I know—"

"Enough to mind your manners in the *earl* of Suffolk's house, surely." Sir Philip cut him off more sharply. Sir Clement drew up short. In that brief advantage Sir Philip said as calmly as before, "May I suggest you and your nephew and ward go to supper quietly now?"

The sideways lift of Sir Clement's mouth was more sneer than smile. "You may suggest. And I may do exactly what I want."

He twitched his head in parody of a bow to Sir Philip, then seemed to notice Frevisse for the first time and bowed more credibly to her, then held out his hand demandingly to Lady Anne. Her chin jerked up and her lips tightened, but she stepped away from Guy, made a curtsy to Sir Philip and Frevisse, and, spurning the hand, left the antechamber. Sir Clement, pointedly ignoring his nephew, followed her. Guy, darkly flushed and silent, bowed in his turn and went after them.

When they were gone Frevisse said, "Despite all that, I have the distinct impression Sir Clement was enjoying himself."

"I'm quite sure he was." Sir Philip turned. The small room's single low-burning lamp was at his back; in what shadowed light there was, the deep pockmarks of his face were not visible, giving him momentarily the handsomeness he would have had without them. But it was handsomeness without expression as he said, "Strife has always been Sir Clement's favorite pastime."

"You know him, then?"

"He did give the impression of knowing me, didn't he?"

If there was amusement in Sir Philip's voice, it was very dry. More than anything, his polite-and-nothing-else tone and expression told Frevisse that he intended—and expected her—to say no more about what had passed between him and Sir Clement.

Matching him in discretion, Frevisse said, "What of his nephew and the girl? There seems to be trouble there."

"It's been a while since I had anything to do with Sir Clement or any of his family. I have no idea what that was about, beyond guesses that you can make as well as I." Now there was very definitely mockery in his tone.

"I daresay I can," Frevisse said. "Though of course we may both be wrong, it being none of our business." She turned back to the chapel to use what little time she had left for prayers. She noticed Sir Philip did not follow her; his place beside the coffin remained empty.

Chapter

5

CARDINAL BISHOP BEAUFORT put aside the last of the correspondence and nodded to his clerk. "Have someone take them in the morning."

With a bow, the man gathered the pages up and carried them away. They would be folded and sealed and given over to a messenger, but none of that need concern Beaufort now he had read them over and given his signature. He was deeply committed to efficiency, and that included having servants he could depend on for minor details.

That nonetheless still left a great deal for him to do.

Beaufort had come directly to Thomas from a meeting of the Great Council. Nothing of importance had been decided, as usual, there being too many factions squabbling for control. Never mind that most of the faction leaders were unable to manage even their own affairs; each had convinced himself and his followers that without him the government would fall into chaos.

So, generally, it was necessary that Beaufort manipulate them with such tact that they failed to realize that he was—far more than they—governing the direction the kingdom went. Able to judge more deeply and assess more broadly than most

men both their needs and weaknesses, he was usually success-
ful.

He had—fully knew and fully admitted to himself that he
had—a drive to power that had taken him now almost to the
limit of his ambitions. But the ability to foresee what others
would do and the effort to bring them to his will was tiring
upon occasion.

Eyes shut, Beaufort rubbed his forehead with his large,
beringed hand. What he wanted right now was time for
mourning, and there was none. He had taken on the main
burden of overseeing the funeral arrangements because he
could see—couldn't anyone else?—that Matilda was
barely holding in one coherent piece. Beaufort thought the
better of her for it. She was a place-proud, tongue-wagging
woman who had longed for the honors her husband had
refused. Beaufort had listened to an amused Thomas's
reasons for rising no higher than an esquire, had accepted
them but never understood them. Matilda had neither
understood nor accepted.

Though their daughter's marriage to an earl and the
prospect of noble grandchildren had soothed her somewhat,
she had never let Thomas forget what he (and she) could
have been.

So her effort to cope with the funeral burden while
keeping silent over her own pain was, in Beaufort's view,
more grace and courage than he had expected from her, and
he had willingly taken as much of the burden from her as he
could.

But it was a burden. With Chaucer gone, Beaufort felt far
lonelier than he had felt since he was a child, when his
deeply kind, endlessly loving, greatly beautiful mother had
gently explained to him the realities of his life—that
nowhere in England was there anyone like himself except

his two brothers and sister, bastard children of the royal duke of Lancaster, fourth son of King Edward III. Had his father married her before their birth—but he could not—they would have had right to the highest places in the realm. As it was, they were barred from any claim to anything not given them by someone else's grace. A grace they were not assured of.

But out of their father's love for their mother, the grace had come. Places in their father's royal household for his two brothers, eventual marriage to an earl for his sister, and for himself what he had longed for most—learning and the priesthood. Oxford, and then the Church, with a bishopric in his early twenties despite his bastardy.

And then long past the time when anyone would have expected it, and to the wonder of all—not least their children—John, Duke of Lancaster, had married the mother of his bastard children. And King Richard II had legitimized them with right goodwill and grace.

But John of Lancaster had died not long thereafter, and his eldest son and legitimate heir, Beaufort's half brother, Henry of Hereford, had set Beaufort a problem that could have ruined him. Henry of Hereford, as arrogant a man as had ever lived, had always quarreled with his cousin King Richard over matters trivial and important. It was not that either was so very wrong, but that they were two very different men. Their enmity had become a fight for the Crown.

Beaufort had been bound to King Richard by temperament, gratitude, and deep oaths of service and loyalty. But there was also the tie of blood to his half brother. And—he would admit in his most private moments—a fellow feeling with Henry's ambition to greatness.

He had gone to Thomas, the one man he could open his

mind to, if not the depths of his heart. Thomas, safely removed from the quandary, had said with warm sympathy, "If you were a less ambitious prelate, you could retreat to your bishop's palace and outwait what they'll do. But you've put yourself too far forward, and you'll have to choose between them or give up any hope of either of them favoring you anymore, whoever wins."

And Beaufort, as nearly always, had seen which way the matter must go, early enough that he had thrown his support to his half brother without seeming to hesitate. He had won that gamble; his half brother had become King Henry IV. Only Thomas had known how hard that decision had been.

And even Thomas had not known how deeply Beaufort had grieved for King Richard's death when it was over with.

But that had not affected his service to the new House of Lancaster on the throne. He had served his half brother to the height of his abilities, and his son King Henry V after him, and now his grandson King Henry VI, Beaufort's own great-nephew, in an upward spiral of prominence and power.

It had not been easy, of course. There had been setbacks, enemies made, repeated frustrations. Through it all, whatever had gone wrong or right, Thomas had been there, nearer to him in mind and abilities than anyone else, the one person left since his mother's death to whom he dared grieve and complain, and receive back sometimes sympathy, sometimes humor, sometimes rebuke, always understanding.

Leaning back in his chair, his elbow on its arm, his hand over his eyes, fingers pressing on his aching eyelids, Beaufort was aware of his servants moving softly around the chamber behind him. Someone would shortly need his decision about something, and he had better be gathering up his wits to give it. And there was supper to go to. Tonight the family would dine in the parlor again, and he must be kind but firm and never in any way disrespect his position.

Then tomorrow there was the funeral and the funeral feast, where he must be even more a pillar of the family and an honor to both the Crown and the Church, whose representative he was. He said a prayer for both his own endurance and Matilda's.

Someone had come to stand silently in front of him, waiting to be noticed. Beaufort drew a deep breath and brought his mind back to the problems of the moment, then dropped his hand into his lap and lifted his head.

It was a relief to see Sir Philip there, who was inclined to talk only when he had something needful to say, and was to-the-point and sensible when he did.

"Yes?" Beaufort asked.

Sir Philip bowed deeply. "I regret the need to trouble your grace, but thought you might want to be forewarned that Sir Clement Sharpe has come."

"Is he in his usual humor?"

"Very much so."

"You've spoken with him, then."

"Been insulted by him and turned the other cheek so he could insult it, too, would be a more accurate description."

Beaufort's mouth quirked with appreciation. "I daresay so. I'll take what steps I can to limit his . . . activities. And Sir Philip . . ."

The priest paused in his bow of leave-taking. "My lord?"

"There has been and there will be little chance to talk through these few days, so I may as well ask you here while we have the chance. What are your plans now that Master Chaucer is dead?"

Two years ago, Thomas, at the death of his household

priest, had asked Beaufort to recommend someone to replace him. Beaufort recommended Sir Philip, a minor member of his own household then, both because of the man's clear intelligence and because of what he had made of his initially limited chances in life.

Priest to a wealthy household was a position a man might comfortably have for life. Thomas had been pleased with him, and so far as Beaufort had been able to learn, so was the rest of the household, to the point where it appeared he could look forward to being priest to the earl of Suffolk now. One of several priests, of course, since the large household of an earl required more spiritual sustaining or more churchly show than a single priest could provide.

Sir Philip tilted his head as if he found the question puzzling and unexpected. "Your will is mine in this, my lord. Of course."

"You have no preference?"

"Only to trust to your judgment regarding where I can best serve."

The answer was impeccable, as everything Sir Philip did seemed to be. But it showed nothing of the man's real desires. With a nod and a small gesture, Beaufort dismissed him. Sir Philip bowed and withdrew, going past Beaufort's shoulder and out of sight toward the door.

Beaufort brooded at the air in front of him for the length of a long drawn breath, then roused with a shake of his head and a grunt at his own unspecific dissatisfaction and set himself to the duties of the evening.

Chapter

6

AFTER ALMOST A month of damp chill and overcast skies, the funeral morning arrived sharply cold under an achingly blue sky.

The funeral procession would form in the outer yard across the moat at mid-morning. Chaucer's pall-draped coffin would be borne on a black cart drawn by black horses in procession to the church in the village, where Bishop Beaufort would conduct the funeral rites and the coffin be consigned to its tomb. Then the living would return to the manor for the feast, and the dead would remain, his soul already gone to heaven, his body to wait for Resurrection Day.

At least with the new, bitter cold, the road would be more frozen, Frevisse thought as she partially opened a shutter in the parlor to see the day. For today, all of Ewelme was shutter-closed in the darkness of mourning, and her aunt's bedchamber and the parlor would remain so for another month at least. But for the moment Frevisse and Dame Perpetua had the parlor to themselves.

In the band of chill sunlight she had let in, Frevisse sat down on a stool across from Dame Perpetua, with cushions from the window seat to kneel on, and began Prime's prayers. Since it was Sunday, the prayers were elaborated from their everyday patterns, but the core remained the same.

"Domine Deus omnipotens, qui ad principium huius diei nos pervenire fecisti: tua nos hodie salva virtute; ut in hac die ad nullum declinemus peccatum, sed semper ad tuam justitiam faciendam nostra procedant eloquia, dirigantur cogitationes et opera."

Lord God almighty, who has brought us to this day's beginning: save us by your power, that in this day we turn aside into no sin, but always go toward your justice; turn our words, our thoughts, and works toward your will.

By God's will. For God's will. In God's will.

But Chaucer, who had been more near to her in mind than anyone else in her life, as dear to her as her own parents, was dead. By God's will, she would never see or hear or laugh or speak with him again in this life that might last, for her, so many more years.

She was crying again. The tears dropped down on her folded hands, warm against her cold skin.

But Prime wove around her its comfort and hope for the day. Her tears were done by the time they finished the office, and she pressed her eyes dry with the heel of her hand before raising her head to smile at Dame Perpetua, not in apology—there was nothing shameful in crying—but in assurance that she was ready to go on with the day. With the wry humor she had shared with Chaucer, Frevisse thought what small sense it would make if she worried over Aunt Matilda's frailty and then fell apart herself. Simple crying was a safeguard against that; it eased the tight band of her grief and let her face the day more coherently.

"Dame Frevisse?"

She turned to see who was speaking to her from the parlor doorway, then rose quickly. "Robert!" She held out her hand for him to come in. The changes she had glimpsed in Robert Fenner yesterday were even more apparent now that she saw him face-to-face. He was a few inches taller than their last meeting, and his boy's lean frame had filled out into a young man's. But he was still Robert, with his engaging, open smile, and he came to bow to her with the same assured competence she remembered in him.

"I was hoping to talk with you sometime before you left," she said. "How goes it for you with Sir Walter? How have you been?"

"He's no worse out of the ordinary." Robert smiled. As a dependent relation of Sir Walter Fenner, Robert was in service to him from necessity rather than choice. "Aside from the fact that he has plans for my marriage, I'm managing well enough."

He said it lightly, but not quite lightly enough.

"Your marriage?" Frevisse asked. "You're of age and you were never his ward, so how does it come about that he should be making your marriage for you?"

"He has a well-landed cousin, a widow who has taken a fancy to me, and if I have any hope of a life above cleaning other people's pigstys, which is what Sir Walter will break me to if I refuse, I'll marry Blaunche the haunch when I'm told to."

"Oh, Robert!"

"But—" Robert held up a hand against her commiseration. "Life isn't doing well by him, either. Lord Fenner recovered from what was supposed to be his final illness— just when Sir Walter could all but feel the lordship in his hands—and now is looking like to live another twenty years." Robert managed to hold his brimming laughter to a wide grin.

Well able to imagine impatient, ambitious Sir Walter's reaction to that turn of fate, Frevisse could not help her answering smile. "So perhaps your wife-to-be is not the worst that can happen to an ambitious man after all?" she suggested.

"She laughs like a tickled crow. And has the brains of one." He turned away abruptly, saying, "Pray, pardon my failed manners. Have you met Jevan Dey yet? He came with his uncle yesterday."

Frevisse had not noticed the quiet young man waiting in the doorway behind Robert until then. He came into the room now and bowed to her and Dame Perpetua. His movements were as angular as his build, though with a precarious grace that might have had charm if he smiled. But his long face did not look as if he ever found anything amusing. Something about his pale skin and plain brown hair and eyes reminded Frevisse of someone. "Jevan Dey," she said. "Would your uncle be Sir Clement Sharpe?"

"The resemblance has been often mentioned," Jevan said shortly.

"And he doesn't much like to hear of it," Robert said, with the glint of humor Jevan lacked. "Sir Clement is a bullying—" He thought better of whatever word he had had in mind and said instead, "We came to know each other the times our lords have met to abuse each other's company. Now when we're alone we abuse them."

"That's neither wise nor charitable, since they *are* your lords," Dame Perpetua said mildly.

"My uncle is neither wise nor charitable, and never scruples to say what he thinks of me," Jevan said. "To anyone who might be listening."

"And more especially to your face," Robert added.

"I've only met Sir Clement briefly twice," Frevisse said, "but I can believe he enjoys sharpening his teeth on other people's reputations. Robert, there are duties I must go to, but if we can speak later . . ."

"At your pleasure, my lady." Both young men bowed and stepped aside for Frevisse and Dame Perpetua to pass.

On the stairs outside the room, Dame Perpetua said, "Unless you need me, I'd like to go to the chapel. I've had hardly a chance to pray for Master Chaucer's soul, and I remember him kindly."

"Please go if you want. There'll be more than enough women around Aunt Matilda by now. Even I will probably be unneeded."

Dame Perpetua patted her arm. "You know better than that. My prayers will be as much for you today as for your uncle."

Frevisse felt the warmth of tears again, and was grateful for the comfort; the living needed prayers as much as the dead. "Thank you."

To her surprise, there were not many people with her aunt. Only Alice and Joan and three maids of the household, and Bishop Beaufort sitting to one side, with Sir Philip behind him, an open prayer book in his hands.

With the shutters closed and everyone dressed in black, the room seemed full of denser shadows moving in the lesser ones of the subdued lamplight. Aunt Matilda was ready except for the padded headroll and black veiling she would wear. Joan, a comb in one hand and pins in the other, had apparently been fastening up her mistress's gray hair, but Aunt Matilda had moved away from her and was standing in the middle of the room saying in a voice thick with nervousness and grief, "How am I going to do this? I don't know how to do this!"

Quickly, Frevisse shut the door. Alice cast her a grateful glance on her way to take her mother's hands that were wringing and twisting at each other. "Mother," she said in a golden, winning tone, "it will be all right. I'll be there with you. And so will Suffolk. You know you can do this. For Father's sake."

"Everything I ever did was for his sake," Aunt Matilda moaned. "And he left me anyway. I can't face his being gone!"

"You can, Aunt," Frevisse said soothingly. "Of course you can."

"I *won't*!" She was clinging now to Alice as tightly as Alice was holding her, but blindly. She was falling into utter panic, and if she did there might be no reaching her for no one knew how long. There was nothing wrong in the widow weeping through the funeral, and surely Aunt Matilda needed the release of tears—she had shed too few of them so far—but for her own sake as well as everyone else's she should not be in hysterics.

"Matilda," Bishop Beaufort said in the deep, rich voice that could fill the reaches of a cathedral but here only spread warmth and assurance through the room, "God is with you. And so are we."

Aunt Matilda caught her breath in the middle of another rising cry, gasped into silence, and stared at him. Bishop Beaufort rose to his feet in a contained and graceful movement and came to her. He took her hands from Alice, engulfing them in his own.

Again, Frevisse was surprised at how large he was and at his control. She suspected his anger was a thing to be avoided at nearly any cost, but he was all gentle strength now as he told Matilda, "You must do this thing, this last, hard thing, for Thomas. He loved you, Maud. He trusted you to show the great lady that you are. We know you'll not disgrace him now."

Aunt Matilda gulped and sniffed and looked up at him, her courage visibly returning to her. Sir Philip came to her side and spoke too low to her for Frevisse to hear, but Aunt Matilda's back straightened further and her face regained its firm shape.

"Of course," she said, and withdrew one hand from Bishop Beaufort's to take hold of the priest's arm. Supported by them, she nodded to her women to complete her for what needed to be done.

Quickly, Joan pinned up the last of her hair, and the maidservants brought first her black wimple, then the padded roll and veil. When they were done, her round, white face was surrounded in the black lineaments of mourning in which her red-rimmed eyes were the only color.

Alice came forward to kiss her cheek, and Frevisse was about to add comfort of her own by saying she was an honor to Thomas, when there was a questioning knock at the door.

Perhaps the marshal, come to say everything was ready in the yard, Frevisse thought, though it seemed too soon for that.

One of the maidservants went to open it, and Frevisse was surprised to see Jevan Dey, his face even more rigid than when he had been with Robert. He bowed stiffly and said without entering the room, "Mistress Chaucer, my apology for disturbing you, but Sir Clement Sharpe asks leave to speak with you now."

"Speak with me?" Aunt Matilda let her disbelief in such a request show. "Now?"

"Surely he knows this isn't the time!" Alice was already past her mother's disbelief into anger.

"He'd speak with you before the burdens of the day accumulate," Jevan persisted.

Frevisse doubted the words were his; he seemed to dislike even the taste of them in his mouth.

"To give his personal condolences on your loss," he continued, "and to assure you he will not ask settlement in the land dispute until your mourning is less fresh, and to ask you speak well of him to the earl of Suffolk in all matters they will have to deal in, now that Master Chaucer is dead."

The impertinence of the words brought everyone but Aunt Matilda to a complete standstill. She clutched at Sir Philip with renewing panic and cried to Bishop Beaufort, "I can't . . . not this morning . . . how . . . how can he ask me . . . how does he think I—"

"Send him away," Alice demanded, hugging her mother around the shoulders. "You don't have to deal with this now. Not ever! Suffolk will see to him!"

"This is nothing you have to endure right now," Frevisse agreed angrily, though not at Jevan, who had plainly wanted nothing to do with what he had had to say.

Bishop Beaufort placed himself between Jevan and Matilda and said, his voice hard with dismissal, "You've done your duty in bringing your master's request. Now you may go. Mistress Chaucer is not free for this matter this morning, as your master well knows. Tell him from me—" Bishop Beaufort stopped. His face went smooth as oil on water, and he turned his attention from Jevan, pale but still facing him, to Sir Philip. Almost genially, he said, "Sir Philip, go with this young man, I pray you, and give Sir Clement this message from me: 'You are a mannerless knave, and if you cannot at least feign some decency in a house of mourning, you are more than cordially welcomed by all here to leave at your earliest possibility.'"

Sir Philip's usually impassive face registered several emotions rapidly. Refusal was perhaps first, but if so he buried it as it was born. Frevisse thought the last was a residue of wry humor for the unpleasantness to come, but even that she could not be sure of before his face became a smooth match of the bishop's. He leaned reassuringly nearer to Aunt Matilda, still desperately clutching his arm. "I'll be gone only a little while, my lady, and be back before you need to go out. But I must obey the bishop in this matter."

With an unsteady sniff, Matilda gathered herself, nodded, and let him go. When he and Jevan had left, and the maidservant had closed the chamber door, Aunt Matilda looked around at all of them and said with something of her old dignity and urge to manage, "Well, I see no point in our all standing about when we could sit. There'll be standing enough today before we're done, I'm sure. Is it very cold out? But never mind, it doesn't matter. Dear Thomas never minded the cold like the rest of us did."

Alice burst into tears.

And Frevisse thought that was the most useful thing any of them could have done, as Aunt Matilda turned from her own grieving to comfort her.

Chapter
⚜ 7 ⚜

"Subvenita, Sancti Dei, occuritte, Angeli Domini. Suscipientes animan ejus: Offerentes eam in conspectu Altissimi."
Come to his aid, Saints of God; hurry to meet him, Angels of the Lord. Take up his soul: Bring it into the sight of the Most High.

The service was making its dark and eloquent way through the Mass for the Dead. The day's sunlight through the bright windows added richness to the elaborate vestments of the priests and Cardinal Bishop Beaufort and strewed jewel colors over the darkly dressed mourners crowded in the nave. Under the growing cloud of incense, the church grew warm with the many people, a warmth welcome after the slow, cold procession behind the coffin from the manor house.

"In quo nobis spes beatae resurrectionis effulsit . . ." In whom the hope of a blessed resurrection dawned for us . . .

Drained, Frevisse let the service carry her as it would. Elegant, complex, the Mass comforted sorrow with the divinely given hope that death was not the end. Even weeping seemed irrelevant for the while.

"Vere dignum et justum est, aequum et salutare, nos tibi semper et ubique gratias agere . . ." Truly it is fitting and just, reasonable and good, for us to give thanks to you always and everywhere . . .

But in some way none of this solemnity seemed anything to do with Thomas Chaucer as she knew him, the man who had always challenged her to think, a man full of laughter and sometimes teasing and often kindness.

But then, in essence, the Mass for the Dead had nothing to do with that part of Chaucer that had been his earthly self, but with the part of him that would live for eternity. The part of him that was now purged of earthly matters and emotions. The part of him she did not know and had not yet learned to love in place of the other who had gone forever.

The pastor of Ewelme began his sermon with the customary reminder, "Behold this coffin containing its dead burden as you would a mirror, for surely you will come to this in your turn. . . ."

Frevisse turned her mind to prayers of her own until the Mass continued.

"Et ideo cum Angelis et Archangelis, cum Thronis et Dominationibus, comque omni militia caelistis exercitus, hymnum gloria tuae canimus, sine fine dicentes: Sanctus, Sanctus, Sanctus . . ." And so, with angels and archangels, with thrones and dominions and all the assembly of the heavenly host, we sing hymns to your glory, without end saying: Holy, holy, holy . . .

Around the altar the priests and deacons moved in their ritual patterns, Bishop Beaufort foremost among them, perfect in every movement and gesture, as if what he did was infinitely precious. As truly it was. But he made it seem as outwardly so as it was inwardly, a rare and beautiful thing to watch and listen to.

Chaucer would have appreciated that, Frevisse thought. He had loved beautiful things, from a delicately swirled and tinted Venetian glass goblet brought from overseas with infinite care and cost, to the subtleties of a sunset over his own hills.

Was there anything like that in heaven for him to love?

Or was heaven all love, with no need or desire distinguishing one soul from another? What was it like, to be pure spirit? And how, without throats, did the angels endlessly sing, Holy, holy, holy? And how did the saints hear them without ears?

"Circumdabo altare tuun, Domine . . . enarrem universa mirabilia tua." I will go about your altar, Lord . . . describing all your wonders.

Chaucer's body was blessed and censed and given at last to its tomb. The last prayers were said, for all the dead, past and to come. The prayers felt as real as a comforting arm, and Frevisse wrapped the words around herself. *"Requiem aeternam dona eis, Domine. Et lux perpetua luceat eis. Requiescant in pace. Amen."* Eternal rest give to them, Lord. And let perpetual light shine upon them. May they rest in peace. Amen.

The mourners eased their way out of the church, into the bright day and cold wind. The sky that had been clear when they entered the church was now streaked with high, thin clouds, and to Frevisse's mind there was the smell of snow to come, or very bitter frost. The villagers were crowded around the church porch, waiting for the funeral alms and to bless the widow and Countess Alice as they came by. Frevisse, behind her aunt, was bemused to find she was expected to walk with Suffolk, an unlikely occurrence under any other circumstances, but at least there was no need to speak to one another, and they did not. She had no good opinion of him, not much opinion at all, though she remembered Chaucer had once said, on a visit to St. Frideswide's after their betrothal, "They're well-matched in wealth and affection, and he has power and she has sense. They should do well enough."

She half expected Sir Clement Sharpe might take the chance between the church and manor house to approach Aunt Matilda. His gall and lack of manners apparently did not preclude such rudeness. But she only saw him distantly among the crowd as they slowed to cross the bridge from the outer yard. His nephew Guy was to one side and there was a glimpse of Lady Anne's fair hair to his other. Let them keep their troubles to themselves today, Frevisse thought, and tomorrow they would be gone with the rest of the guests.

Once inside the manor house, they came into the hands of Master Gallard. Today the usher's main task was to oversee the sorting of everyone into their proper places along the outer sides of the long trestle tables set facing each other in a double row the length of the great hall, from the high table on the dais at the hall's upper end to the screens' passage at its foot. Among the matters Aunt Matilda had fretted over yesterday had been the question of whether there would be enough room for everyone, but the time of year, and the weather, had held back the number who came. There was room enough, though barely.

The principal problem—and one Frevisse was glad fell onto the usher Master Gallard and nowhere near her—was of precedence. The family and those guests of very highest estate would sit at the high table. The tables down the hall would seat the guests of lesser rank. To seat them in precedence, giving offense to none, was a delicate art and a diplomatic balancing act. Master Gallard, fussy and over-busy as he always seemed to be when facing far less trying tasks, managed with surprising skill. For this occasion of rigorous importance, his fussing had smoothed over into competent haste. And haste was very necessary in directing servants to guide guests to their places all around the tables before there could be impatience or open complaint. He had committed everyone's face and place to memory. There was no order to their coming, but as they reached him at the door into the hall, he directed the servants where to lead them with a gesture and briefest word. In remarkably short while, the guests were seated along the outside of the tables, and the servers were bringing out the first course of the elaborate meal.

Frevisse, as a member of the family, had place at the high table; but because she was not of Chaucer's actual blood, she was at its far right end, well away from the concentration of lordliness at its center, where Bishop Beaufort, as a prince of the church and great-uncle to the king as well as Chaucer's cousin, held pride of place next to Aunt Matilda, with Alice on her other side. Not even the duke of Norfolk, sent as the king's representative with the royal condolences, had precedence over Bishop Beaufort, and Alice's husband, as earl of Suffolk, was further aside, beyond the bishop of Lincoln.

The high table was nearly the width of the hall itself, and crowded full with others almost as impressive as those at its center. But Frevisse, overly warm in the church, then chilled during the windy walk back to the manor house, and now growing too warm again in the crowded hall, was more concerned that she might have a headache coming than with conversing with any of them. She was not used to headaches and was not sure if her head's ache was going to increase into something sickening or ease as she grew used to the crowding and noise—even at a funeral feast, the talk rose loudly with the need to be heard over the voices of so many others. But since she was at the table's end, there was no one to her right, and the abbot on her left was far too busy talking toward the more important center of the table to pay more than passing heed to her. Except that they shared serving dishes and a goblet between them, he would probably not have acknowledged her presence at all.

To her wry amusement, Frevisse found herself caught between annoyance at being ignored and relief that she did not have to bother with conversation more complex than, "Yes, thank you, I'll have a little of that." She ate meagerly, but mostly her attention wandered to the guests at the long tables below her among the bustle of servers. She saw Dame Perpetua, well down the other side of the hall, seated with another nun and Sir Philip and a man who was either bald or another priest; it was difficult to tell at this distance.

Somewhat nearer along the tables, Frevisse recognized Sir Clement Sharpe with Lady Anne and his nephew Guy on either side of him. Keeping them apart still, Frevisse thought, and wondered how much good it would do him in the end.

Leaning over Sir Clement's shoulder to pour wine into the goblet he shared with Lady Anne, was Jevan Dey. Seen together with his uncle, their resemblance was marked. But where Sir Clement's face was active, open and intent, Jevan's was shut, without even the small animation he had had when talking to her with Robert Fenner. Sir Clement had much to answer for there.

Because of the excess of people, a great many of the guests were being served by their own servants or, if their estate was sufficient, their own squires. There was an almost constant flow of food from the kitchen, entering from the screens' passage and spreading out along the inner side of the U-shape the tables made. The platters and bowls of everything from wheat hulled and boiled with fruit to capons stuffed with oysters were arranged to serve people by fours, except at the high table, where in token of their place only two shared the served dishes. That meant Frevisse received some attention from the abbot beside her, as he displayed his manners by setting particularly choice bits on her plate before taking his own portion. Still unsure of her head and of how her stomach might respond to so much rich food, Frevisse ate only what she felt she absolutely must—a chicken wing, a modicum of dried fruit seethed in wine—until the oyster stuffing; she forgot herself with that and ate as much as might be. She could not remember when last she had had oysters.

The next course was pies full of beef and currants, their juices dark with spices and orange peel. Each was surrounded by baked eggs, and Frevisse, her appetite roused now, cracked one and ate it. That left her mouth dry and she drank deeply from the goblet she shared with the abbot, wiping her lips first so that no grease might sheen the wine, wiping the rim afterwards where her lips had touched. As she set the goblet down, the abbot took it up and drank deeply enough to empty it, without bothering to wipe lip or rim; apparently thirst was more than manners with him. Frevisse averted her eyes from his lapse and refrained from comment as she let him place a share of the pie on her plate.

While she ate, her gaze moved absently around the hall. She caught glimpse of Robert Fenner serving a little ways down the table in front of her, but did not see Sir Walter. Dame Perpetua was speaking with Sir Philip, their heads close together to be heard. Sir Clement, she saw, was shifting a fistful of bones from his plate to the voiding platter in front of him that showed he had taken the greater share of the chicken that should have been split equally among him, Lady Anne, Guy, and the man beyond him. So he was greedy as well as contentious. How many other sins did he so fully indulge in? Frevisse wondered. She watched with amusement as Lady Anne drew him into conversation over the goblet they shared while Guy drew the large custard Jevan had just set before them toward himself and gave large portions to himself and the man beside him.

Then someone moved directly in front of her, blocking her view but bearing a welcome pitcher of wine. Frevisse glanced up in gratitude—she was thirsty again—then said with outright pleasure at the familiar and friendly face, "Robert! What are you doing?"

"Waiting on you, my lady, and anyone else between the whiles Sir Walter needs me. He's down the tables from you only a little way, in heavy talk with an archdeacon over the cost of masses for the dead. Look—no, you can't see him for the fat justice of common pleas in the way, and he can't see you—"

"Which should help both our digestions," Frevisse put in.

"True," Robert agreed. He set the goblet back on the table, filled to a neat margin from the rim and, still leaning forward, asked too low for anyone else to hear in the general loudness of the hall, "How is it with Lady Thomasine?"

"She's Sister Thomasine these three years," Frevisse said gently. "And it's very well with her. She's happy."

"God keep her so," Robert said, and went away down the tables to fill other people's goblets.

Frevisse said softly, "He does." She took the goblet before the abbot's hand reached it, to drink deeply enough both to satisfy her thirst and to leave him waiting for another server to satisfy his own. There were ways of being rude that were far more polite than his.

But her thoughts stayed with Robert. Three years and he still remembered a love he had known barely three days, had never had any real hope of even then, and had never seen since. Was it truly love with him? Or only the longing after Love that settles for the lesser thing, fixing the heart on something of the World because to fix the heart on the Thing Invisible that was the core and creation of Love in its full reality took more courage than many wanted to give to their lives.

Frevisse's own choice had been made before she was Robert's age, and she still barely had an answer for herself, let be anyone else.

She became aware of a disturbance down the hall, heads turning toward rising voices and servers drawing back from one part of the tables.

"Now, pray, what is this bother?" the abbot said in distaste.

"Sir Clement Sharpe," Frevisse said, seeing the center of the trouble.

"Ah, yes. Of course," the abbot agreed, unsurprised, and reached for the new plate just set down before them laden with minced meat shaped like pears and gilded with egg yolk touched in one place with cherry juice to heighten the illusion, with a fragment of almond for a stem. Frevisse ignored the plate to watch Sir Clement, on his feet shouting at the man on the far side of Lady Anne, who was also on his feet and shouting back at him. The general noise of the hall was too great for Frevisse to understand what they were saying, but Lady Anne was cowered down between them, while their near neighbors were crowding away along the benches from whatever was going to happen. Except Guy, who, behind Sir Clement, was rising to his own feet and reaching out to his uncle's shoulder.

Realization of what was happening had spread through the entire great hall now. Conversations died into a hush just as Guy gripped Sir Clement's shoulder from behind and Sir Clement turned on him, knocking his hand away and shouting, "Keep your hand off me, you murderous young whelp!"

Then Sir Philip was there, gesturing Guy back while interposing himself between Sir Clement and the other guest. Aware of how many were straining to hear him, he spoke low, first to Sir Clement and then to the other man. Guy had subsided onto the bench again; Frevisse saw him and Lady Anne exchange looks and Guy shake his head, all unseen by Sir Clement who was now arguing with Sir Philip.

Or beginning to, because as Sir Clement leaned his face into the priest's, his voice rising again, Sir Philip made a small but definite gesture past him toward the high table in forcible reminder of where they were and who was watching.

Frevisse doubted Sir Clement needed reminding; again he gave her the impression of a man exactly aware of what he was doing, and enjoying it. But Sir Philip's gesture gave him excuse to straighten, swing around, and make a flourishing, apologetic bow to everyone at the high table, and another to the widow and Bishop Beaufort in particular. Then he caught up the goblet from between himself and Lady Anne, held it high, and declared in a voice that carried end to end of the great hall, "But if I'm wrong in this matter, may God strike me down within the hour!"

As dramatically as he had bowed to the high table, he downed what was in the goblet in a single toss, set it down with a defining clunk on the tablecloth, looked all around at everyone, and sat down abruptly, straight-backed with pride and enjoyment of every eye on him.

"He's always doing that," the abbot observed for Frevisse's ear alone. Through the hall a broken murmur was passing, people bending to explain something briefly to one or another, and then voices rose again in ordinary talk.

But Frevisse, still shocked to the heart by Sir Clement's words, turned to the abbot. "What did you say?"

Cutting into his illusion pear, the abbot said, "He's always doing that. Swearing he's right and may God strike him down within the hour if he's not. Someday God may oblige him, and he'll be quite surprised."

A server set a dish of minted peas in front of them. The abbot lost interest in her again.

Robert returned to pour more wine. "Don't look so horrified, Dame Frevisse. Almost anyone who's been around Sir Clement more than half a day has heard him say that."

"But it's blasphemy, daring God that way! And to do it so casually—"

"But it's dangerous only if he's wrong, and Sir Clement never believes he's wrong."

"What of the poor girl, caught in the middle of all that? How long until she comes of age and is rid of him?"

"Lady Anne is as vulnerable as a hedgehog," Robert said without malice. "All soft eyes and gentle ways and a thousand spines. Whichever of them marries her, he won't have as lovely a time of it as he thinks he will."

He was moving away as he said it, and gone too far for Frevisse to ask who besides Guy wanted to marry the lady. But it was hardly a difficult guess. The angry moments outside the chapel had revealed Lady Anne's relationship with Guy; and by his fury it would be no surprise if Sir

Clement were interested in marriage with her, as well. Of course he had the upper hand in the matter because while she was his ward he controlled her marriage. He could not, by law, force her to marry against her will, but the law also provided severe penalties for her if she refused a reasonable match. And there were subtler ways than the law to make her life a hell and bring her to his will, if he chose to take it that far.

Frevisse took a deep draught of the wine. Her head was surely tightening itself into a headache, and there was at least another hour left to this feast. She regarded her illusion pear and the dish of peas with distaste; she was used to far simpler food at St. Frideswide's and had already eaten more meat than would usually come her way in a week. Later her stomach would certainly have something to say about the rich assault she had made on it.

There was another commotion from where Sir Clement sat, and people were again drawing rapidly away from him, this time Guy and Lady Anne among them, so that very suddenly Sir Clement was alone, still seated but bent forward toward the table with both hands clutching at its edge as, red-faced with effort, he strangled for breath.

"Well!" said the abbot. "Perhaps God's grown as tired of him as the rest of us have and decided to judge him after all."

Chapter

8

After the first moment of shock, the hall seethed into chaos, with some shouting, a few screams, and much exclaiming. People rose to their feet, some trying to pull farther away from Sir Clement, others crowding toward him. A few climbed onto benches, craning for a chance to see, and fragments of prayers rose among the exclamations, inquiries, and frenzied chatter. Sir Clement was blocked from Frevisse's view, but like the abbot, she kept her seat, knowing futility when she saw it; even with the added height the dais gave to the high table, she would see nothing if she stood. There was nothing she could do at this distance, no way to get through the turmoil to Sir Clement. But she crossed herself and began a fervent prayer for him, because he was clearly in God's hands now and for him especially that must be a terrifying place. Very rarely was God's judgment seen so clearly, swift and sure, in this world. With that fear on her, she added a prayer of acceptance of his will, because God forbid she contradict him in his judgment, lest in another way she be as guilty as Sir Clement.

Beside her, she noticed, the abbot was deep into passionate prayer of his own.

Down the hall some sort of order was being forced.
People shifted back so that a few men—mostly servants,
but Sir Philip among them—could help Sir Clement to his
feet and away from the table. He was bent far over, still
strangling for breath, his fists pressed hard against his chest.
Crying, "Make way!" the men holding him up half led, half
carried him from the hall. A momentary silence followed
them, but when they were gone the babble of wonder and
alarm began to rise again.

Bishop Beaufort rose in his place to his full, impressive
height and, with his hands held wide to include everyone in
front of him, declared in his strong voice, "Good people!
We've seen a wonder here with our own eyes. May God,
having made his will manifest, have mercy on this man. Let
us pray for him. And for ourselves, who may be as near and
unknowing as Sir Clement was to God's great judgment.
Return to your places, I bid you. Sit, that we may pray."

He was so completely sure of their obedience that—
scared or awed or wary—people complied, the guests
subsiding onto their benches, the servers to their places near
their lords or along the screen to the kitchen. The gap where
Sir Clement, his ward, and his nephew had sat remained
eloquently empty; people glanced at it and nervously away,
or kept their eyes averted entirely.

Bishop Beaufort waited until the hall was still and all
their eyes on him. Then he brought his hands together, said,
"*Oremus*," and bent his head. Every head in the hall bent
with him, and in a voice that carried all through the hall,
meant to reach everyone as well as God, he said, "Lord of
power and might, may we—dust in your wind—learn not
to tempt your wrath. If it be your will, spare Sir Clement
Sharpe, that he may be a better servant in your sight to the
end of his appointed days, if these be not they. *Sed fiat*

voluntas tua. And may we all come to the ends you have appointed and find your mercy at the last, through Christ our lord, who lives and reigns forever. Amen."

He lifted his head and said in a more common voice, "Now let us remember that we came to honor our friend Thomas Chaucer and go on with this meal in remembrance of him, may he rest in God."

A murmurous response ran through the hall. Hands moved, making the cross from head to breast, left shoulder to right. Some heads remained briefly lowered in personal prayers. Much subdued and in deep order, the meal continued. Bishop Beaufort sat down and turned to comfort Matilda, pale and shaken beside him.

Frevisse gave up anything more than the pretense of eating, and with her headache did not dare drink more wine. Robert did not return, and the abbot made no more effort at conversation. Left to her thoughts, she did not like their morbid turn; God so directly manifest against someone who had tried his patience past endurance was not a comforting sight. She took her mind away from the incident, sheltering in watching other people down the hall.

Two servers were clearing away the dishes from Sir Clement's place. One righted a goblet and dropped a towel over a wide wine stain.

Farther down the tables, Dame Perpetua had stopped eating and, very white-faced, sat with bowed head, lips moving in silent prayer. The nun sitting beside her was weeping and telling her beads. Sir Philip had not returned, and a large woman had shifted sideways to take advantage of his vacated place.

The next course, roast pork on a bed of saffron rice with apricots and mushrooms, was just being set in front of her and the abbot, when her aunt's lady-in-waiting Joan leaned

over her shoulder and said low in her ear, "My lady and
Countess Alice ask if you would mind going to see how Sir
Clement does, and return to tell."

"Assuredly," Frevisse said. She could leave the table with
less disruption than anyone else, she supposed, and her
report would probably be more detailed than a servant's.

Aside from those considerations, she welcomed an excuse to leave the hall. She rose and asked, "How is it with
my aunt?"

Joan shook her head and made small tch-tch-tch sounds.
"She's being very brave, despite the fright that fool gave us
all. She'll see the day through well enough, but there'll be
payment tonight and afterwards, poor lady. Valerian would
help her rest if she'd take it, but she always refuses. You
might speak to her about that, my lady, if you would."

"I will," Frevisse said as Joan curtsied and returned to her
mistress. With a murmur of apology to the abbot, Frevisse
excused herself, leaving the hall by a door behind the dais.
She stopped a servant in the corridor who said that Sir
Clement had been taken to the priest's room above the
chapel.

Among the benefits of being priest in a household as
large and rich as Thomas Chaucer's was a private room for
sleep and prayer and study. It was a sensible place to have
taken Sir Clement; it would not inconvenience any of the
family, was well out of the way of other guests, and could
easily be closed to the curious.

A narrow, dark, steep stairway went up from the chapel's
antechamber and opened directly into the priest's room. It
was the same size as the rich chapel directly below it but
austere, with everything in it, even the cross above the
prie-dieu against one wall, plain or old or both. There was
an aumbry along one wall for storage, a bare wooden table,

a single chair, one joint stool. A narrow bed was along a wall, with a servant's truckle bed under it and gray woolen blankets on it. Only the rug underfoot gave the room any color, and it was obviously a castoff from some other part of the house, its patterns faded and muddled with wear.

This barrenness was not Chaucer's provision for his priest. Frevisse remembered coming to make confession here when she lived at Ewelme. There had been a colorful hanging, a gaudily painted crucifix, and a far bigger bed with a bright coverlet. This austerity must be Sir Philip's choice, but she noticed that the one fine piece of furniture was a tall desk, set to catch the best light from one of the two narrow windows, and the only sign of wealth were the books on the shelves behind the desk's footrest. It was a scholar's desk, meant and used for work, and had, in contrast to all else in the room, a completely superfluous and beautiful fretwork of wood deeply carved and swirled between its legs.

Frevisse absorbed all that in the first moment she reached the doorway, then focused on Sir Clement. He was not lying on the bed but seated at the table, leaning forward over it, his hands braced on its edge, and all his concentration given to his breathing, which was clearly easier than it had been when he was taken from the hall. Near the further window were Guy and Lady Anne, he standing rigidly, she close to him, one hand on his arm, the other pressed to the base of her throat as if to hold down her fear. Jevan Dey stood alone, nervously rubbing his hand on his thigh.

Sir Philip was beside the table, and behind him waited a plainly dressed man Frevisse took to be his servant. Directly opposite Sir Clement, the doctor—to judge by the cut of his dark gown—was bent down and staring broodingly into his face, concentrating on Sir Clement as if concern alone might be enough to cure him.

Suddenly Sir Clement shoved himself upright, to draw a deep, wheezing breath. The doctor and everyone else started. Frevisse smothered a gasp. The man's normally lean features were not only bloated but viciously patterned with irregular red welts across his cheeks and down into the opened collar of his houppelande.

But in a voice still recognizably ill-tempered, though thickened, Sir Clement demanded, "A drink. Even water. Something."

The doctor looked at Sir Philip and nodded, and the priest gestured at his servant who moved toward the aumbry as Guy turned to look in its half-open door, then reached to take out a long-necked bottle.

"That one, yes," Sir Philip said. "And the cup, too."

Looking annoyed at Guy's intervening in his duties, the servant brought out a pottery cup while Guy pulled at the bottle's loosened cork.

Sir Clement, his breathing still ragged, glared at the doctor, then shifted his gaze past him to Guy and Lady Anne. "Not yet," he grated. "You won't have her yet." Lady Anne's hand tightened on Guy's arm, holding him back from a harsh move forward. Sir Clement looked at Jevan; his mouth quirked cruelly. "Live in hope and die in despair, boy. I'm still here."

Jevan's eyes darkened with deep anger. Lady Anne shook her head, warning him to keep back whatever he was about to do or say. Whether for that, or out of his long habit of control, he held silent and still. But the anger remained in his eyes.

"Here." Sir Philip took the filled cup from Guy and made to offer it to Sir Clement.

But Clement made an inarticulate noise and began to fumble frantically at the wide cuff of his houppelande's long sleeve, loosening it and then pushing it as far up as it would go, to let him come at the red rash covering his arm. "Hell's fire! I'm being spared none of it!" He began clawing his fingernails at the rash. The doctor put out his hand to stay him. Sir Clement left off scratching long enough to shove him in the chest, forcing him back a pace, growling, "Leave me be!" Then he seized the cup from Sir Philip, snapping, "Give me that!"

He drank all the wine down in clumsy gulps, flung the cup at the table, and began to dig at his arm again.

From a safer distance the doctor said, "You should try to lie down now, my lord. To rest. I—"

"Ass! I can't . . . breathe . . . lying down." Sir Clement's breath caught and fought among the words. He struggled and it broke loose with a snoring sound. He wheezed a few deep breaths to catch up his air and sat with his head cast back, eyes shut. A thin rivulet of drool ran unheeded out of the corner of his mouth. Around him, everyone stood motionless, eyes fixed on him.

After a few moments, when nothing changed, the doctor said in a whisper, as if that would keep Sir Clement from hearing him, "He's better than when he came from the hall. There's that for hope."

"But you don't know what it is?" Sir Philip asked.

The doctor cast him a dark glance. "It's not like anything I've seen, no." In a lower whisper, almost between his teeth, he added, "It wouldn't be, would it?" *Because who among them had seen God strike down a sinning man before?*

Sir Clement reared his whole body back in his chair in a sudden terrible struggle for air again. His upper lip had shaded to blue; his eyes were staring with panic at nothing—or at nothing anyone else in the room could see in front of him. Then, with his fists clenched and his forearms pressed against his ribs as if to force air out, he lurched forward to lean across the table in much the same way he had in the hall when the first attack came on him.

The doctor and Sir Philip and the servant closed on him as if there was something they could do. Jevan, grabbing the wine bottle from Guy's hand, came to snatch the cup from the table and fill it. Belatedly Guy followed but only a few steps, keeping his distance from his uncle. Lady Anne stayed where she was, her hands pressed over her mouth, looking more a child than ever in her wide-eyed fear.

Sir Philip drew back a step now and made the sign of the cross over Sir Clement, large enough to include his servant and Jevan and the doctor all together. The doctor gestured Jevan's cup away. He was trying uselessly to straighten Sir Clement to see him better. Sir Philip crossed himself and began to pray in Latin.

Frevisse and everyone else there crossed themselves in response.

How long Sir Clement's struggle to breathe went on Frevisse could not have said. Forever. And not long. The tortured gasping turned to a high wheezing and then guttural choking. Frevisse, raising her bowed head as she prayed aloud for mercy, for pity, saw Sir Philip turn from the table to the aumbry. He was still praying, too, his lips moving silently now while his hands did something out of her sight. Then he turned back to the table with a glass vial and a piece of bread in his hands, and Frevisse realized what he held and what he was going to do and sank to her knees.

Pushing Jevan and the doctor aside, he bent over Sir Clement and said loudly at him, "Do you repent? Do you ask for the body of your Savior and repent of all your sins?"

Belatedly everyone else in the room saw and knelt, even the doctor, though he was last, resisting the end that had to come.

Sir Clement's body shuddered with the struggle for breath, but Frevisse was able to see his now desperate nod to the question that could mean his soul's salvation. Sir Philip forced the small bit of bread into his mouth, poured oil—the blessed chrism—from the vial onto his own fingers, and drew a cross on Sir Clement's reddened, swollen, shuddering forehead. His eyes staring and mouth agape with the uneaten bread in it, Sir Clement fixed his gaze on Sir Philip, who stayed bent over him, face close to face, praying at him until Sir Clement's head fell back, his mouth now working soundlessly, his eyes suddenly fixed on the ceiling for an ugly, drawn-out moment before they went sightless and he slumped in the chair, still staring upward but his eyes empty now of anything alive.

Then Sir Philip said, *"In manus tuas, Domine, commendo spiritum eum."* Into your hands, O Lord, I commend his spirit. The hoped-for last words of every Christian that Sir Clement had not been able to say for himself.

Chapter

9

THE DAY HAD been longer and worse—in several ways—than Beaufort had anticipated. Seated at the table spread with work in his chamber, daylight fading to gray half-light but no lamp lighted because he had not yet given the order, he rubbed his forehead in what he knew was a habitual gesture. He was tired, but there were matters to see to so messages could go at first light tomorrow morning, matters that could not be delayed because they concerned both the government and his bishopric, and neither of those could be left to themselves for long.

On the whole, his bishopric was the lesser problem—and the more profitable—since he had appointed men that he could—not trust; trust left one too vulnerable—but men he could depend on to see that things were done the way he wanted them done, and to let him know if for any reason they could not.

England's government, being less under his personal control, was far less well-ordered. The reasons for that were almost as numerous as the men who felt they had a claim to the right to advise young King Henry VI, men who could never be brought to see that "claim" and "ability" were not necessarily the same thing. His deservedly detested, much deplored nephew Humphrey, duke of Gloucester, came first to mind. For the present the duke was as circumvented as could be managed, though the complete cessation of his interference in the government was not even to be hoped for.

Blast Thomas! He had been one of the few men Gloucester respected enough to listen to. Not necessarily heed but at least be slowed on whatever half-brained scheme he might have at the time.

But Thomas, except for brief occasions, had refused to be dragged into the coil around the King. And now he was beyond any part in it at all.

Beaufort made a prayer for Thomas's soul. He had kept as emotionally distant from thinking about Thomas as he could today; it was easier to deal with matters competently if emotions were kept out of them. He would pay for that restraint later, he knew, with probably a week's ill temper, but it had seen him through the day's necessity. Now he put Gloucester firmly out of his mind, too. Even merely thinking about Gloucester was a profitless, aggravating waste of time. What needed to be dealt with here and now was a far lesser matter than the King's royal uncle, but at least it was one about which something could be done, Beaufort hoped.

One of his secretaries knocked once at the open door across the chamber. Beaufort nodded for him to come in and, seeing Dame Frevisse and the nun who had traveled with her behind him, rose to his feet. "Dame Frevisse. Thank you for coming so promptly."

He held out his hand. The two women crossed to him, curtsied, and kissed his ring. Then the second nun withdrew to stand near the door, head down, hands folded into her opposite sleeves. It would be unseemly for any nun to be alone with a man, but she was politely removing herself as much as might be. Beaufort glanced around at the two clerks working at tables along the far wall; they were out of earshot if he and Dame Frevisse kept their voices low.

He indicated she should sit on a stool beside the table. "I hope my summons was not too inconvenient. You are undoubtedly tired after such a day."

"At your pleasure, my lord bishop. There is no inconvenience." She sat straight without stiffness, her hands, like her companion's, tucked into her sleeves, her voice pleasant, mild in the middle range.

Beaufort studied her face in its surround of white wimple and black veil and learned no more about her. She was here, obedient to his summons, as anyone would be. Whatever she felt or thought about it did not show. That in itself told something about her: not many lesser people came into his presence without showing something of unease or overeagerness, depending on what they feared or wanted from him. Did she fear nothing? Want nothing? He remembered her sudden push for information about the availability of affordable grain the evening their paths had first crossed—and how that one sign of interest in his power had, at the mildest possible rebuke from her aunt, been withdrawn completely. But even in that brief exchange he had sensed her strength of will. Thomas had been right; she was an unusual woman, intelligent and controlled, no matter how meekly she sat here beside him, eyes modestly downcast, waiting for him to speak. *Very well.*

"Your uncle charged me with a message for you as he lay dying."

Her head came up, confronting him with a look that was neither meek nor modest but sharp as a hunting hawk's. But her voice was steady as she said, "Yes, my lord?"

Watching her carefully, Beaufort said, "He said to tell you he would miss you."

She bent her head too swiftly from him to read her reaction, and for perhaps a dozen heartbeats she was silent, then said softly, her face still lowered, "Thank you, my lord."

"I believe you will miss him?" He made it a question, so she would have to answer.

She lifted her head. There were tears in her eyes, but she said steadily, clearly not caring that he saw, "He was my friend. I have no other like him. And never will."

Beaufort looked away, reached out and drew a bundle toward him across the table. "He also left you this, a bequest outside his will, to do with as you choose."

He held it out to her. As she took it, he noticed how long and fine her fingers were, and though she was too strong-featured to be commonly beautiful, her face was not unattractive. Thomas had said she had freely chosen to be a nun and never shown herself discontented with her choice, but still the bishop wondered why she had made it when certainly she could have married well enough. Thomas would surely have given her a dower, fond of her as he was. Beaufort had had occasion to wonder about other nuns' choices through the years, choices that, like Dame Frevisse's, puzzled him.

She set the bundle on her lap and placed her hands over it. Though the gesture was quiet, her hands seemingly at ease, Beaufort had the intuition that it would cost a battle to take it back from her, should anyone be so foolish as to try.

"You're not going to open it?" he asked.

"Not now," she said, her composure complete, her look directly into his eyes asking what concern it was of his. When he did not respond, she dropped her eyes, waiting to be dismissed.

Pleased to disconcert her, Beaufort leaned back in his chair and said, "Well, I have a request of my own for you."

He thought he detected a wary stiffening in the pause before she looked at him again. But her voice was as even as before. "Yes, my lord?"

"There was a death here today. You witnessed it, I believe."

"Yes, my lord."

"And you were distressed by it."

"I've seen death before, my lord. I'm never glad of it but . . ." She hesitated, then said, "But it's a part of life. It comes to us as surely as birth. To be angry at one is to be angry at the other."

"And both come at God's will."

"Yes, my lord."

"And this particular death, it's being said, came more directly than most from God."

"Yes, my lord."

"I want to be certain of that."

Dame Frevisse opened her mouth as if to protest but remembered herself. "How can you be more sure than by having seen it with your own eyes? He wished God's judgment on himself and it came."

Beaufort knew what was being said throughout Ewelme manor house and—by this time—in the village, and what would be said much farther afield as guests went away to their own homes more full of the talk of Sir Clement's death than of Thomas's funeral. God had worked a wonder in the sight of everyone there today, and it would be more than a nine days' wonder.

"I want to *know* that that is what it was," he said.

With some asperity behind her continued respectful tone, Dame Frevisse said, "Then I suggest you ask Sir Philip. He was nearer to it than I from the beginning, and with him to the very end of it."

"I have already spoken with Sir Philip."

And been thoroughly unsatisfied because the priest had seemed as willing as everyone else to accept God's hand in Sir Clement's death; had seen no further, asked no further, wondered no further than that God chose that time and place to make his power manifest. "Your uncle told me you have a way of finding out things that others do not see."

Dame Frevisse drew a deep breath as if to speak, but then tightened her mouth and said nothing. Instead, she bowed her head, hiding her face again.

Beaufort went on, "I want to be assured this was indeed an uncommon death. I want to be sure of God's will."

Dame Frevisse straightened to look directly at him and asked a question he had not expected. "Why?"

He could simply require her cooperation out of obedience to his place as a prince of the Church. But with memory of things Thomas had said about her, Beaufort leaned forward, dropped his voice to make this clearly between only the two of them, and said with the plain truth, "I want to know if there was man's hand in this, and sin. Sir Clement was a blaspheming man for many years. I doubt there's anyone could count now how many times he's stood up and said, 'If I'm wrong in this, may God strike me down within the hour,' but it was often and often without God ever taking notice of him. I've heard him myself, on occasions enough when his lies were baldly apparent to all present. So I can't help wondering why God would choose to strike him down now in particular, when there were other, more suitable times. Unless one is inclined to think God was asleep or busy elsewhere on the other occasions."

Dame Frevisse's mouth twitched with an effort against

smiling. It was a gesture Beaufort had often seen on Thomas Chaucer's face. "I didn't know it was that way with him," she said. "Only that he seemed to enjoy creating angers around him."

"Oh, indeed he enjoyed that," Beaufort agreed. "And that's what makes me wonder about his death. He had a talent for garnering enemies, and made a practice of never losing one once he'd gained him. But what I want to know particularly . . . is whether or not Sir Philip had a hand in it."

His words startled her, and she did not try to hide it. "Sir Philip? Why do you suspect him in particular?"

"I don't, in particular, suspect him. I simply want to be sure I don't have to suspect him at all." Beaufort hesitated; but she was an intelligent woman and would serve better if he made himself clear. "I have had my eye on Sir Philip these few years. He, like you, has abilities beyond the ordinary, and I'm ever in need of such men in my service. But I need men I can be sure of before I put them into offices where I must trust them. 'The king ought to place in posts of command only those of whose capacity he has made trial.'"

"'And not to proceed to make trial of the capacity of those whom he has placed in posts of command,'" Dame Frevisse immediately answered, completing his quotation. "Vincent de Beauvais. And very true."

So she was as knowledgeable as Thomas had led him to believe. Very learned, Thomas had said, and had not added, For a woman. Beaufort wondered what the book in her lap was, that Thomas had so particularly wanted her to have.

But that was not to the point. Permitting himself a smile of appreciation for her completion of his quote, he said, "Exactly. So I would know whether Sir Philip is a murderer or not before I begin to trust him."

"There was . . . strife between him and Sir Clement?"

"Sir Philip is freeborn, but only barely. His father was still villein to Sir Clement's father when Sir Philip was born, but Sir Philip's mother was a free woman and he was born on her freehold property and is therefore free from birth himself, according to the law. His father later bought his way out of villeinage and, with his wife's property and help, became quite prosperous and provided both education and opportunities for his sons. Sir Philip in particular took best advantage of the possibilities, and looks to go far in the Church. But Sir Clement had been making claim that he had proof Sir Philip is not freeborn after all, is still, in fact, a villein and therefore Sir Clement's property. If Sir Clement had pursued and proved such a thing, Sir Philip's future would have been severely hampered."

"But Sir Clement had not pursued it into court yet?"

"And curtail his sport? The torment of the uncertainty of his victims was among the things he most enjoyed."

"By your words, he had more victims than Sir Philip," Dame Frevisse said. "Sir Philip won't be the only one who might be glad to have him dead. Possibly he's not even the only enemy who was present at the funeral feast."

"Most assuredly. Now mind this: Sir Philip does not know how much I know about him. He only knows we both agreed Sir Clement was a pain better avoided if possible. So when you begin questioning people about Sir Clement and his death . . ." Dame Frevisse raised her eyebrows at the word "when." Beaufort did not care. She was going to do this thing for him, whatever she thought. ". . . he will have no reason to suspect you are especially interested in him, since you cannot know there was especial reason for him to want Sir Clement dead. Do you understand?"

Chapter

10

FREVISSE FOUND THAT on closer acquaintance she did not much like Bishop Beaufort. Nor the way that he was watching her across the little distance between them with the remote calculation he would probably give to a property he was thinking of investing in. And she doubted he cared that she was watching him as warily as she would an adversary about to make a threatening move. He did not care, she thought, whether a person liked or disliked him, so long as they did what he asked. And did it well.

What had Chaucer told him about her? Why would such a powerful man ask this of her? In a cool, level voice that she hoped matched his own, she said, "I understand and will try to do as you wish, my lord bishop."

Bishop Beaufort nodded, then made a graceful gesture of dismissal. He would always be graceful in success, Frevisse thought, and wondered how he was in defeat. She rose, made low curtsy to him again, and left. Dame Perpetua silently followed.

Interested and speculative looks were turned on them by people in the outer room, but Frevisse walked through without raising her head, the cloth-wrapped bundle pressed against her middle by her folded hands, her veil swung forward on either side of her face in appearance of holy modesty.

In truth she was feeling nothing remotely like holy, and just then modesty was the least of her concerns. But she wanted no one to speak to her; she did not trust her ability to answer well or even politely. She wanted to be alone, to think how best to do what Bishop Beaufort was asking. With the instinct of her years in St. Frideswide's and her knowledge that with Ewelme crowded with guests tonight there was no private place to go to, she retreated to the chapel.

In its antechamber, as Frevisse reached for the door handle, Dame Perpetua touched her arm, stopping her. "Dame Frevisse, how is it with you?" she asked gently.

Frevisse turned to her. "How much did you hear of what he asked of me?"

"All of it, I think. Will you be able to do what he wants of you?"

It had been for her common sense and good manners that Perpetua had been chosen to come with her; nor did Frevisse have any doubt of her discretion. But this was not something she thought she could share. "I don't know," she said, her voice sharpened with her own desire not to be burdened with the problem. "I don't even know if I know how to try." She reached for the door again. "I need to pray awhile."

Behind her, Dame Perpetua said quietly, "Prayer is meant to be a strength and guidance, not a hiding place."

Frevisse paused as the justice of that warning struck to the soft core of her conscience. She had no reply. Her darkness was her own, and God had not yet shown her the way out of it. Until he did, prayer was her only ease. And her only guidance. She did herself that much justice: she was searching for a way out of the darkness of her regret, a way through forgiveness—God's and her own—into acceptance of her deeds, not into escape from them, or denial. And prayer was the only way she had. Prayer was not her hiding place but her hope.

But that was not something to be put into words here and now. After a moment, not answering Dame Perpetua, she went on into the chapel.

Sir Clement's body was laid out where Chaucer's body had been yesterday. There was no coffin yet; the body, completely enveloped in a white shroud, rested on boards set on trestles covered with black cloth, seemly enough until a coffin could be made. His relatives would depart with the body tomorrow, Frevisse supposed. No, the crowner still had to come, as he always did, to investigate any uncertain or violent death. Neither Sir Clement's body nor his family would be able to leave until then, and there was no way to know yet when the crowner would arrive.

She crossed to the far side of the chapel, Dame Perpetua behind her. It was dim here, well away from the door and from the light of the few candles set around Sir Clement's bier. She recognized Jevan kneeling at the head of the coffin, his face above his clasped hands touched with the warm golden candlelight. Three others, one of them Master Gallard, the usher, by his shape (but subdued and motionless for once), knelt in a row beside the coffin, facing the altar, their backs to her. In a hush of skirts, Dame Perpetua sank down to her knees beside her. Frevisse followed her onto the familiar hardness of stone floor, bowed her head, folded her hands together—and found that instead of going readily into the comfort of prayer, she was staring blindly at the floor in front of her, thinking of the problem she had been set.

There was no question but that she must do as Bishop Beaufort had asked. He was her religious superior, and there was nothing immoral or illegal about his request. Though St. Frideswide's Priory was in the bishopric of Lincoln, not his of Winchester, he was still a bishop and moreover a cardinal, and his power and influence stretched where he wanted them to in England. If she failed to obey him, she might suffer for it in some way. But if she tried and honestly failed, she thought he would accept her failure without blame.

But the problem remained of how to attempt what he had asked.

He doubted Sir Clement had been struck down by God. Why? And why did he believe it possible that Sir Philip had murdered him? He wanted to know what had happened because he had plans for Sir Philip and wanted to be sure of him. Sure that he had not committed a murder—or sure that he had? her mind treacherously suggested. She was not sure Bishop Beaufort had made that distinction clear when he asked her to learn the truth.

But at least he had given her the priest's possible motive. The threat of villeinage was a heavy threat to hold over a man. And yet Sir Philip had been singularly undisturbed by the insults Sir Clement had thrown at him yesterday, as if neither they nor Sir Clement particularly mattered to him.

Or had he been hiding his true reaction with exceptional skill?

And if he or someone else had killed Sir Clement, how had it been done?

Poison was the obvious answer. The doctor would have spoken out about any wound, and there had been the strange struggle to breathe, as if Sir Clement were being throttled by an invisible foe, and the swollen face, the rash, and the red welts.

But how could he have been poisoned? Sir Clement, like everyone else, had shared his food and drink. Lady Anne and Guy had shared his food; she and Sir Clement had shared a goblet; yet only Sir Clement had sickened.

Even if in some way it had been poison, Sir Philip had been well down the table from Sir Clement at the feast. Except that once, when he had come to quiet Sir Clement's outburst, just before Sir Clement had called down God's judgment on himself. Had Sir Philip goaded that from him? Perhaps, but as nearly as Frevisse could remember, he had not been close enough to the table to have put poison into any food or drink. But perhaps, if it was poison, it had been given earlier. What else had Sir Clement eaten or drunk? Breakfast, surely. Was there a poison that was so slow to act?

Or perhaps the poison had come later. Sir Clement had been the only one to drink the wine in Sir Philip's chamber, just at that point where he had appeared to be recovering. What if God's hand had touched him but not closed on him, only leaving him with warning of his sinful mortality and an opportunity to change? Had Sir Philip—or someone else, Frevisse added conscientiously—taken the chance of what was meant to be God's warning on Sir Clement to kill him?

The poison had worked swiftly there in Sir Philip's room, with symptoms seemingly identical to those that had struck Sir Clement in the hall. And since no one could have foreseen God's action, how would they have had a poison so readily to hand, and one that matched so well?

She would need to talk to the people who might know or have seen more. And ask the doctor his ideas on the nature of Sir Clement's death. Doctors always had ideas; ever insecure in their inevitably lost battle against mortality, they generated theories as readily as a master smith made weapons.

But whatever she did, whatever she asked, the matter came back to the question of whether Sir Clement had died of God's holy will or man's sinful intent.

A darkness came between her and the candles, and she looked up to find Sir Philip an arm's length away, looking down at her.

She glanced toward the bier and saw the empty place where he had been kneeling. She had been so distracted with her problem when she entered that she had not realized the taller man beside Master Gallard had been Sir Philip.

Now he bowed his head to her slightly, in acknowledgment of her noticing him, then tilted it to one side, asking her to come with him.

She would have to talk to him sometime; at least this way he had sought her out, and so might be less guarded with his answers. With a sense of duplicity, because she had not been praying, Frevisse briefly bent her head and crossed herself, then rose to go with him from the chapel. Dame Perpetua followed her and in the antechamber, as they drew to a far corner, she stopped by the door, her hands quietly in her sleeves, her head bowed, just as she had been with Bishop Beaufort.

With no waste of words over any greeting, and not even a look at Dame Perpetua, Sir Philip said, "His grace the bishop wished to speak with you."

"And did," Frevisse answered, sure he already knew it. What he probably wanted to know was why, but she had her answer ready. "He had a message for me from my uncle. My uncle charged him with it on his deathbed, and he wished to give it to me personally."

"God keep your uncle's soul," Sir Philip said. "And that was all?" His gaze dropped deliberately to the bundle she still held against herself, then returned to her face.

Her expression bland, Frevisse said, "What else should there be?"

Matching her tone, he said, "Your uncle spoke of you upon occasion. He was fond of you. More, he valued your intelligence."

Frevisse bent her head humbly, as if to disparage the compliment, and said nothing.

"And I think he spoke of it to Bishop Beaufort, too."

"That would have been very kind of him," Frevisse said.

"His grace the bishop is not content that Sir Clement's death was God's will."

Frevisse could not help a start of surprise. "He isn't?"

"Didn't he say so to you?"

"Did he to you?"

"He questioned me about every particular I observed of Sir Clement's attack and death, and I don't think he was satisfied with my answers."

"Why? What did you tell him?"

"You saw it, along with everyone else in the hall and then in my room."

"But you were closer. And I didn't see what happened in your room until I came at almost the end."

Sir Philip gestured impatiently. "You saw enough. He was better, able to breathe with less effort and talking lucidly. And then he was struck again and died. You saw that."

Frevisse nodded. She had seen that. She wished she could more clearly remember where the others had been around the room, what they were doing before the second attack, what their faces had betrayed of their feelings. She crossed herself. "As if God had begun to remove his hand from him, and then struck him down after all." She shivered with memory. "Did he say anything before then that I didn't hear? Anything so unrepentant, or . . ." She hesitated. ". . . so blasphemous there was no salvation for him?"

"There was no repentance or fear of God in him at all. He was himself, ill-tempered and demanding as always." Sir Philip paused, then added, "Perhaps that was what brought God's final anger down on him. That even so plainly warned, he saw no error in his ways."

Drawn along that path of thought, Frevisse quoted, "'What, do you think your life was given to you forever, and the world's goods with it?'"

"'Nay, nay, they were only loaned to you, and in a while will go to another,'" Sir Philip answered.

It was a game Frevisse loved, and she was good at it; but this time she had to admit, "I know the quotation but don't remember the source."

"It's from *Everyman*," Sir Philip said. "I've never seen it performed, but your uncle had a copy of it."

The chapel door opened quietly on its well-oiled hinges, and Jevan Dey came out. He paused at the sight of them, then closed the door and bowed. The lamplight in the antechamber was as dim as yesterday, but where its shadows obscured Sir Philip's ruined face, they deepened the tense, exhausted lines around Jevan's mouth and eyes, making him look more nearly his uncle's age than his own. "My lady," he said to Frevisse, then turned to Sir Philip. "I thank you for giving my uncle his final absolution. We were all too . . . stunned to ask for that. For his soul's sake, my thanks. If he comes to peace at last, it's by your hand."

"And God's will," Sir Philip said. "But for your kind

words, thanks." He gestured toward the chapel. "I'll pray for him whenever I can."

Jevan's smile was taut. "There'll be few others who'll come willingly. He made himself disliked. And his death has made people afraid even to be near his corpse."

"At least there's someone with him now," Frevisse said.

Jevan shrugged. "I doubt prayers will aid his soul. If ever any man was damned directly to hell, it was Sir Clement. But he appreciated the forms. When it suited him. My own presence beside him this while is the last thing he can require of me."

He chopped his sentences as if following a thought all the way through were difficult for him. It was weariness rather than grief lining his face so deeply, Frevisse decided.

Sir Philip said, "But you can go rest now, can't you? You've done enough for this day, I think."

"I want to find Guy. He should be here, too. For form's sake, if nothing else. He's Sir Clement's heir."

"And you?" Frevisse asked. Jevan was Sir Clement's nephew, too, and surely heir to something.

Jevan's attempt at a smile made sharp, unamused angles in the lines around his mouth. "I'm Sir Clement's dog. If he had his will in this, I'd have my throat cut and be buried at his feet. That would have pleased him more than my prayers."

He was too tired for any pretense, Frevisse thought, or for clear thinking. Food and rest and the wearing off of shock would be the best things for him now. As he bowed and moved to leave, she said, "If you see Robert Fenner without Sir Walter near"—Jevan would understand—"please tell him I'd be glad of a chance to talk with him once more before he leaves."

"Certainly, my lady. My lord." He bowed to them again, and left.

"If you'll pardon me," Sir Philip said with a bow of his own, "I'll go with him, I think, to be sure he eats and does indeed sleep tonight, rather than coming back here to pray again."

"He had no fondness for Sir Clement, so it's doubly to his credit to do what he's doing," Frevisse said.

"But that makes it no less tiring. Doing right from a sense of duty is more wearing than doing it from affection."

"And so has greater merit."

"Truly," Sir Philip agreed. "By your leave, my ladies." He bowed and left them.

To Dame Perpetua, still silently standing to one side, Frevisse said, "I suppose we should go to Aunt Matilda now." For her, in this, affection and duty together were going to be equally wearing; she wished someone was going to bid *her* have her supper, then go to bed and be done with the day.

But no one was likely to. Resigned to that, she led the way toward her aunt's parlor.

Robert Fenner met them at the foot of the stairs. "Jevan said you wanted to see me," he said, with no more greeting than a quick bow and a glance over his shoulder toward the hall. "Sir Walter is not pleased to be among those left to each other's company in the hall. He hoped for a chance to talk with his worship, the earl of Suffolk." His tone caught both Sir Walter's arrogance and his own ridicule of it.

"And lacking that pleasure, he's spreading his discontent wherever he best can," Frevisse said.

"As ever," Robert agreed. "So I can't be gone long."

Understanding the hint, Frevisse asked directly, "What do you know about Sir Philip's relationship to Sir Clement?"

"The priest? Your uncle's household priest? Nothing."

"It's said his father was a villein of Sir Clement's father. Basing, I think the name was."

"Ah!" Robert nodded. "I know the common gossip there. Basing bought his freedom with his wife's money, and then went on to increase her small fortune to a larger one and set the sons he had by her in places well above villeinage."

"Sons?" Frevisse asked.

"Two of them, if I remember rightly. The priest and another one. I don't know about the second one. But I do remember talk that Sir Clement liked to claim the purchase from villeinage had not been valid and that father and sons were both still his property."

"The father is still alive?"

"I think not."

"But both sons are alive."

"I suppose so. I haven't heard otherwise."

"And how valid is this claim of Sir Clement's?"

"Probably not at all or he would have pursued it, I suppose. Or maybe he had more pleasure in holding the claim over the sons' heads, threatening to bring it down on them whenever he chose and meanwhile enjoying drawing out the torture?"

"Not a pleasant man."

"You've only to know what he's done to Jevan to be sure of that."

"What has he done to Jevan?"

"Everything where he should have left him alone, and nothing where he should have done something. Sir Clement's sister married less well than Sir Clement thought she should have and completely against his wishes. It might have been all right if her husband had lived long enough to make good on his small inheritance. By all accounts he was clever and capable enough, and he looked to be becoming a competent wool merchant. But he died with his affairs all tangled in investments that needed his close eye, and without him, when all was said and done, there was little left. His wife barely outlived him, and Sir Clement seized on Jevan. There were relatives on the father's side who would have taken him and been glad of it, but Sir Clement had rank and power, and he's used Jevan like a servant ever since, to punish him for his mother's 'sin' in going against Sir Clement's wishes in her marriage."

"But he's still Sir Clement's nephew. He'll inherit something now, surely."

Robert shook his head. "The properties are all entailed in the male line. Everything goes to Guy because his grandfather was Sir Clement's father's brother, if I remember it rightly. Sir Clement reminded Jevan of his lack of expectation frequently and with pleasure."

"God is too merciful; he waited too long to strike Sir Clement down," Frevisse said, then quickly crossed herself. "God forgive me."

Dame Perpetua crossed herself, too; but Robert said, "You're not the only one who's said that, nor do I doubt you'll be the last."

"I saw him die," Frevisse said. "I at least should be more careful of my words." But at the same time her mind was beginning to trace a path among the things she had been learning. "Then Guy is some sort of cousin to Sir Clement, not a nephew. And he's cousin to Jevan, too. Will he deal more justly with him than Sir Clement did?"

"I gather that Guy despises him for a lickspittle, never mind Jevan had small choice in the matter. Jevan has no hopes from him. Or from the other way, either."

"The other way?"

Robert smiled sadly, with memories of his own. "Lady Anne, Sir Clement's ward. Jevan has never said it directly, but you have only to watch him to see he cares for her. I doubt she knows. Between her love for Guy and her fear that Sir Clement might take her for himself, she's had little time to think of other loves. But that's over now, God be thanked, and she and Guy will be free to marry, I suppose. Poor Jevan is out of everything, but it's a suitable enough marriage, all ways—in rank and fortune and affection."

Remembering what she had overheard and seen among the three of them yesterday, Frevisse said with some gentleness, "So Sir Clement's death is boon to Lady Anne and Guy at least."

"And to a great many others," Robert said. "He dearly loved trouble for its own sake. Good my lady, I have to go back or there'll be trouble for me and not of Sir Clement's making."

"Go quickly. I'm sorry I kept you so long. And thank you."

"You're very welcome." He smiled again; Frevisse could remember when there had been real joy in his smile, not this pretense he made of it now. "Pray for me, my lady."

Frevisse, who rarely touched anyone, took hold of his arm for a moment, her eyes on his to make her words go more deeply. "Always. Go with God, Robert, whatever happens."

He bowed too quickly for her to read his expression, caught her hand in his own and kissed it, then turned and left without lifting his gaze to her again.

"I'll pray for him, too," Dame Perpetua said in the silence after he was gone.

Frevisse nodded. "He's in need."

"As are we all." Dame Perpetua's simple certainty let what seemed too easily a mindless platitude be the plain truth that it was.

Frevisse felt suddenly grateful for Dame Perpetua's quiet, steady presence.

Chapter

11

DAME PERPETUA LEFT Frevisse at the door to the parlor. "I am not needed here, nor do I want to go in. I'd rather go to bed, by your leave." Wishing she could go with her, Frevisse gave Dame Perpetua the small bundle to take with her, out of the way. Frevisse had guessed by its feel that it held a book and was curious what Chaucer had so particularly wanted to give her. But she meant to find a better time and place to open the bundle than now and did not wish to draw attention to it by carrying it with her into the parlor. She drew a deep breath, then went in.

The room was even more full of people than the evening she had arrived and, like then, most of them were strangers to her. Aunt Matilda and Bishop Beaufort sat near the fireplace, with Alice at her mother's side and her husband Suffolk at the bishop's, all in low-voiced conversation with various guests. Master Gallard, hovering just inside the door, bowed to her and said under the general murmur of conversation, "My lady your aunt has been asking after you. You'll go at once to join her?"

Eyes kept modestly down, Frevisse eased her way around the edge of the room and people. The conversation she overheard as she went was mostly general, about the wet summer and the small harvest, a new cut for houppelande sleeves, a fragment of an anecdote about Chaucer, an admiring comment on his son-in-law Suffolk. Only once did someone mention death in her hearing, to be quickly cut off by his companion with a nod her way, so that she was not sure whose death he had spoken of. It seemed that here at least politeness was holding back avid talk within her hearing about Sir Clement, and she reached her aunt without being drawn into conversation with anyone.

Matilda, gray with grief, reached out to take her hand and draw her down to kiss her cheek in greeting. "Thank you, my dear, for coming to my comfort. I know you've had a difficult day, too."

Frevisse kept a warm hold on her hand. "Is there anything I can do for you?"

Matilda drew her nearer to whisper in her ear, "Find a way to end this soon." She smiled wanly as she spoke, because they both knew that the evening, like the day, had to take its course. Tomorrow all the remaining guests would leave, and the family could settle to finding their places in their grief. In the meanwhile, the present necessity of gracious hospitality had to be endured. Frevisse squeezed her hand in sympathy and moved to stand behind her, next to Alice, to become part of the polite flow of condolence and comments of people coming to speak to the bereaved family. She avoided even a glance at Bishop Beaufort.

Near the widow there were only kind words about Chaucer or mild reminiscences of happier times shared with him. But from where she stood, Frevisse easily saw the occasional excited hand movement or scandalized head-shaking mixed with uneasy but avid looks quickly curtailed.

It was no more than she had expected. They had seen a

man call down God's judgment on himself and then receive it. Because it had fallen on someone so obviously worthy of his terrifying death, they could afford excitement rather than fear, and indulge in righteous discussions of God's wonders.

Frevisse's gaze flickered sideways and down to Bishop Beaufort's profile to the left of Alice. His voice and subdued movements were perfectly suited to the occasion, shaded to the finest degree of dignity and sorrow. To watch him was to believe there was nothing on his mind but the comfort of the bereaved and courtesy to their guests.

Frevisse knew better. He had succeeded among the harsh realities of the royal court for most of his life; he must perceive a great deal more of what went on around him than others did, and understand it more deeply than most would find comfortable to think on or to live with.

But her uncle had counted Bishop Beaufort not just as his cousin but as his dear friend. It had not been their abilities that differed but their ambitions. Chaucer, knowing how much she would need them, had trusted Beaufort with his last words to her. She had always trusted Chaucer more completely than she had ever trusted anyone else. And he had trusted Bishop Beaufort.

Assuredly the bishop was correct that Sir Clement's had been an odd death. God could take life in any way he chose, and it had become so common to see his will in any unexplained or sudden death that churchly scholars had been obliged through the centuries to point out that not all such deaths came directly from God's hand. But even so, why had this death been given this way—not simply the agony to breathe, the red disfiguring of his face and arms, the final strangling—but that strange relenting before the end, as if God had given only a glancing blow at first and then, when his warning was not taken, when Sir Clement showed no sign of comprehension or repentance, struck the fatal one?

Was that the right of it? And had it been done here, at Ewelme, in front of so many people, to be a public example to other sinners? But most of the people who saw him first struck down had not seen him die, so the example had been weakened, if example had been intended.

A shifting of people near the door brought her gaze around to see Sir Philip entering. He paused just inside to speak closely to Master Gallard, the little man nodding repeatedly to whatever the priest was saying before answering something back. Sir Philip shook his head, touched the usher's shoulder as if in reassurance, and went out again.

Frevisse glanced at Bishop Beaufort to see his eyes shifting away from the doorway. By his bland facade, he might have seen nothing of interest, except his eyes slipped sideways to meet hers, as if wondering if she had seen them, too; then he was answering some comment from the earl of Suffolk as if he had never had his attention anywhere else.

Looking over his head and across the room, Frevisse glimpsed the physician who had attended Sir Clement's death. With an abrupt wish for something besides fruitless speculation, she slipped sideways away from Matilda and Alice and made her way through the crowd toward him. He moved away to talk with another man as she neared him, but she followed to the room's far end and stood a little aside from them, her head modestly down and her hands folded into her sleeves in an attitude of waiting, where he must surely notice she wanted to speak to him.

But overhearing their conversation about the weather and their relief that the chance of plague was gone now that the weather had turned cold, she remembered his name and was able, when he turned from the other man to her, to say,

"Master Broun, I was wondering if I might speak to you about—"

His gesture of recognition interrupted her. "You're Master Chaucer's niece! My pardon, lady, for not knowing you sooner. Of course. Of course. You couldn't ask your aunt about it, could you? Pardon us, please," he added to the other man, who bowed his head and moved away, leaving them in what would pass for privacy in that gathering. Master Broun leaned his head nearer to her and dropped his voice to consultation level. "You're wondering how it was with your uncle, of course. It came on slowly; he had time to prepare himself while we tried all that could be done but, alas"—he spread his white, well-tended hands in resignation —"it was not God's will he live. But the end was peaceful. Very peaceful."

He was an echo of Aunt Matilda. She had repeated and repeated that his end had been peaceful, as if for reassurance to herself more than anyone, so that Frevisse had resisted asking for details that might mar her aunt's comfort. Now, with this unexpected chance, she asked, "Was he painfully ill?"

"Not painfully. Never painfully, no, except for a while when the starvation became marked, but that abated as his decline progressed. You know he fell ill early in the summer? The first indication of trouble was that he lost flesh with no cause. He seemed in good health but no matter what he ate, he lessened. We began to do all manner of things that should have helped." He shook his head, his expression puckered with professional regret. "But nothing we did realigned his humors."

If he were like others of his kind Frevisse had known, he would go on now to lengthy and detailed discourse on bile and sanguinity and the courses of the stars before he came back to the plain fact that Chaucer had died despite all his doctors' knowledge and care. To forestall him, she said, "So it was a wasting disease, not painful in the main but with no hope."

"Not by late autumn. From then it was merely a matter of time." He spread his hands again in token of helplessness in the face of fate. "An unusual case, but not unheard-of."

"And the man who died today, Sir Clement Sharpe. What happened to him?"

The physician stared at her blankly for a moment, then remembered to shut his mouth, only to open it and say rather severely, "You were in the hall, I believe? Yes, then you saw him. He called on God to witness his truth, and God smote him in his lie. And you were there in the priest's chamber when he died. My lady, you *saw* how he died."

"But he didn't simply stop living," Frevisse pressed. "It wasn't that simple. I saw what agonies he was in—"

"Certainly." Master Broun was beginning to be offended.

Frevisse moderated her tone to humble inquiry. "It was so terrible to see. I couldn't watch. He didn't choke on a bite of food, or the wine he drank go down the wrong way? It's so terrible to think of God striking him down in that manner. I just keep hoping it was something else, and if it was, you would be the one who knew."

Her double appeal to his learning and his manhood flattered the physician enough to consider her question. "I of course checked him immediately for some cause of his distress," he replied with suitable gravity, "but there was no sign of what it might be. It was as if all his humors had turned violently against him all at once."

"There seemed to be something in his throat."

"I looked there first, of course, but it was not something *in* his throat, it was his throat itself. A severe and prolonged spasm of all the flesh in there that caused an effusion of fluid and brought on a swelling that inhibited his breathing."

Inhibited his breathing to the point of death, Frevisse thought drily, but she kept her tone mild and wondering as she said, "What about those terrible welts all over his face, and that redness, and the itching that seemed to torment him almost as much as his breathing? They had nothing to do with his throat constricting, did they?"

Master Broun shifted uneasily, then said, "They were no part of his throat's affliction. They were something else altogether, brought on, I believe, by his general distress and the imminence of death."

"His death agonies brought on welts and itching?" In all the deaths she had seen or ever heard of, there had been nothing like that.

Master Broun held silent a moment, uneasy rather than offended, and then said in a much lower voice, "They were no direct part of his throat's affliction. Of that I'm sure. But did you see the pattern of welts on his face, as if he had been struck by an open hand? A hand of more than human size, one that struck and made those marks on him."

Frevisse hesitated. She could not remember any pattern to the marks on Sir Clement's face, but she had been farther away than Master Broun. Had anyone else seen it? Letting that go for now, she asked, "Why do you suppose his breathing eased the way it did? His breathing was much easier when I came in."

The physician was clearly on more comfortable ground with that issue. "There you have further proof of God's work in this. There was no reason for the abatement of Sir Clement's agony for that little while except God's mercy, that he have time to repent. When he did not, his life and soul were wrenched from him as you saw."

Master Broun crossed himself, and so did Frevisse, but as she did, she said, "He drank something just before that final attack."

"Wine. A little wine."

"He didn't choke on it? His throat wasn't still too constricted for it?"

"I would not have allowed him to drink if it had been." Master Broun grew haughty again. "No, Sir Clement did not choke on wine or anything else. It was simply God's will and beyond our comprehension." He spread his hands, indicating even he was helpless before such power. "God's ways are strange to man."

Chapter

12

WRUNG OUT, FREVISSE had thought her sleep that night would be heavy, but it was shallow and broken, rarely deep enough for dreams or long enough for any rest. Dame Perpetua slept through her uneasy stirring, but they had promised each other that if either woke near the time, she would awake the other for the prayers of Matins. Among all the other wakenings there was no way to tell when one was midnight, but at last, wakening yet again, she guessed the time was nearly right and gently roused Dame Perpetua. Together, in whispers, they said the office's many psalms, the soft sound of their praying almost lost in the general murmur of other people's breathing and Joan's snoring.

When they finished, Dame Perpetua lay down, rolled on her side, and was shortly asleep again. Frevisse, still uneasy with her own thoughts, took longer, and in the morning was no nearer to satisfaction or answers—and felt no more rested—than when she had gone to bed.

And Aunt Matilda had finally given way to her grief. She awoke and, as was always her way, rose and went to kneel at her prie-dieu for first prayer. But there, where comfort should have been greatest, she bent forward over her prayer book, shaken by sobs. At first the other women left her to cry; she was past due and surely needed the tears. But it went on, and worsened, until she was clinging to the prie-dieu, helplessly wracked and unable to stop.

As Frevisse hovered uncertainly, Alice left the gown her maid held ready to put on her and went to her mother. Taking her gently by the shoulders, she helped Matilda to her feet and, not bothering with words, led her back toward the bed. Aunt Matilda, her face collapsed and splotched, clung sideways to her daughter and went on sobbing helplessly.

It took so long to calm her that it was a while before Frevisse was free to leave the bedchamber. There had been some thought that she would accompany her aunt and Alice in standing in the hall to bid farewell to the departing guests, but word had been sent to Suffolk that he must take the duty, which was acceptable, he now being Lord of Ewelme, and since Alice meant to remain with her mother, there was no seemly reason for Frevisse to join him.

No one questioned when she and Dame Perpetua withdrew as they had done yesterday, to say Prime in the parlor. And when they had finished, she asked Dame Perpetua, "Will you help me with something?"

Dame Perpetua looked up from shaking straight the folds of her skirts. "If I can," she said. "What is it?"

"About Sir Clement's death."

Dame Perpetua's expression showed her discomfort with the doubts which Bishop Beaufort had expressed, and she said with less confidence, "What do you want me to do?"

"If it wasn't God who killed Sir Clement, then it had to have been poison. I need to know what kind it could have been."

"But Sir Clement shared every dish, just as we all did.

And his goblet, too." Dame Perpetua moved immediately to the same objections Frevisse had to the problem. "How could he have been poisoned and no one else?"

"If we can learn what poison it was, perhaps we'll know. There may be something among my uncle's very many books that would enlighten us. Would you help me look?"

The frown drawn between Dame Perpetua's brows disappeared. Books were her worldly passion, and there were very few of them at St. Frideswide's Priory. But she subdued her obvious eagerness and despite a sudden shine in her eyes said with quiet agreement, "Yes, surely, I'll help you all I can."

Chaucer had found he could deal with his business better the farther he was from his wife's domestic concerns, and so the room from which he had run his merchant ventures and other dealings was at the far end of Ewelme's range of buildings. While they went, Frevisse explained what she wanted. "I talked with the physician. He says Sir Clement died of a cramping of his throat and an effusion of fluids. His throat constricted and strangled him."

Dame Perpetua made a small, distressed sound. It was expected she would be upset by the very thought of such a death, but she was also a clearheaded woman; she would be of more help the more she knew, rather than cosseted in ignorance.

Frevisse went on, "But he didn't just simply die. You saw him choking in the hall, but when I saw him a while later, in Sir Philip's room, he was so much better I thought he was going to live."

"What?" Dame Perpetua asked incredulously.

"The strangling had subsided to the point where he was sitting up, able to talk a little, even drink some wine."

"He was that much improved?"

"Except that he had broken out in red welts over his face

and neck and arms, and their itching was tormenting him."
Frevisse deliberately did not mention Dr. Broun's assertion
that the welts were patterned like an open hand. She wanted
someone else's observation on that and did not want to
distract Dame Perpetua with something she was not sure of.
"Then soon after he drank the wine, the choking came back
and he died, with barely time for the last sacrament."

"God have mercy on him. You think there was poison in
the wine?"

"I don't know. That's the trouble. I don't know anything
that would kill someone the way Sir Clement died. That's
what I hope to find in my uncle's library—something about
poisons that cause those symptoms. The strangling and
welts and unbearable itching."

After a moment of considering that, Dame Perpetua said
very quietly, "Oh my." And after another moment of
thought: "Then you think his worship may be right and Sir
Philip did murder Sir Clement?"

"I don't know clearly yet what to think. But I've begun to
wonder why God would kill a man in so elaborate a way,
instead of more directly, simply, there in the hall as example
to all."

"Dame Frevisse! You're questioning God's will? Even at
the orders of a cardinal bishop that's so perilous! How can
you—" Dame Perpetua gestured in wordless distress at the
plight of being caught between God and the order of a
prince of the Church.

"I know. But what if it *wasn't* God's will? What if Bishop
Beaufort is right and it was a man's will in this? Or if God
did indeed strike at Sir Clement, there in the hall, not to kill
him but only to warn, and someone took advantage of it to
poison him?"

"Surely God would strike down in his turn anyone who dared do such a thing! It would be blasphemy!"

Frevisse refrained from saying God never seemed overly prompt in striking down blasphemers in these days. Like other sinners they seemed to flourish far longer than their deserving. Instead she said, "I'd be more than glad to leave the matter to him. But Bishop Beaufort has directed otherwise. Dame Perpetua, this is my burden, not yours. If you would rather be left clear of it, it's your choice and I'll understand."

Dame Perpetua straightened, her face firm, her hands tucked purposefully up her sleeves. "No. You asked for my help and I'll gladly give it, along with my prayers to keep us safe. And I don't suppose there's blasphemy in what we're doing, since we only seek to understand God's will more clearly, to his greater glory and our salvation. Besides, I want to see your uncle's books."

Frevisse had feared the chamber might be locked, but the door handle gave to her touch and the door swung easily open. With a mixture of emotions she did not try to sort out, she faced the place that, for her, had been Ewelme's heart.

The room was narrow but long, and despite the years since she had last been there, all its furnishings were familiar. She remembered Chaucer saying with amusement at his wife's everlasting desire for change, "I bought what I wanted and needed at the start. Why should I change when they are still sufficient to me? Let my room be."

His desk was set where the light would be best over his shoulder from the windows with their wide seats, where Frevisse had sat reading for many an hour, lost to her proper duties and deeply happy. Chaucer had gathered books all through his life, beyond the considerable number he had inherited from his father. They had long since passed the bounds of being neatly closed away in a chest. He had given over one wall of his room to aumbrys for them, where they were safe behind closed doors but easily reached. Even then, they had always overflowed through the room, and Frevisse had been free to read what she chose, and Chaucer had gladly discussed or explained or argued at length anything that had puzzled her or caught her interest.

In this room, in her uncle's company, she had had a freedom she had had nowhere else in all her life, except in her love of God.

A remembered figure straightened from his bent posture over an open chest across the room. Master Lionel, her uncle's clerk. Frevisse was glad she had seen him several times the past few days so there was no surprise at his white hair, stooped shoulders, and wrinkled face. He had been only in late middle age when she lived here; now he was old. He peered at her across the room through magnifying lenses held on his nose by leather thongs looped around his ears before saying, "Frevisse. Come again," as if it had been only hours since she had last been in his way and he was no more pleased now than he had been then. He had never approved of the time Chaucer had spent on her, to the neglect of business that was the heart and soul of Master Lionel's existence.

"*Dame* Frevisse," he corrected himself. And added, "He's gone, you know. He isn't here."

"I know." Startled, Frevisse responded with instinctive gentleness. Her uncle had not particularly mentioned Master Lionel during his last few visits to her. She wished now that he had, because more than Master Lionel's appearance was changed. "But may I come in? He always welcomed me here."

Master Lionel looked around the room as if searching for

a reason to refuse her, as if certain there was one there. "What do you want? He's gone."

"My friend has never seen his books. I wanted to show them to her."

"It's all right, Master Lionel. I'm sure she's welcome here."

Intent on the elderly clerk, Frevisse had not noticed Sir Philip standing in the contrast of shadow at the room's farther end and partly obscured by an open aumbry door. He came away from the bookshelves now, still speaking to the old clerk. "You can go on with your work. I'll see to them. Master Chaucer would welcome her, you know. So shouldn't we, also, in his name?"

Master Lionel swung his head from Frevisse to the priest, then to Frevisse again and back to Sir Philip. The effort seemed to confuse him. He shrugged. "As you think best." He turned back to the chest, and Sir Philip motioned for Frevisse and Dame Perpetua to come in.

He faced the shelves and pointed at various volumes as if they were what he spoke of, as he said, low and brisk, "He's outlived his wits. It started about two years ago, but Master Chaucer wished him happy and found things for him to do, since he's happy here."

"He still works?" Frevisse asked.

"No, but he thinks he does. He's supposed to be putting the papers in that chest in order and listing all the ventures they pertain to. They're all only draft copies, so it doesn't matter if he shifts and shuffles all day, every day, and scribbles nonsense on that great roll behind him and never gets any forwarder. Can I help you?"

"It's only as I said. Dame Perpetua would be glad of a chance to see my uncle's books, to spend time here if she could."

"And you would not mind seeing them again either."

"This was my best place to be, before I entered St. Frideswide's," she answered, for the first time wondering what he knew of her from her uncle and, more to the immediate point, how they would look for what they needed with him at hand. There were far more books here than she remembered; of course Chaucer had gone on adding to his collection after she left. Nor did she have any idea where any particular books might be. Chaucer had loved to rearrange and reclassify his treasures; she had helped him do it often enough to know that, so there was no telling where anything might be now. A great many of them were spread and stacked in no order at all around the room, used at some time and not put back. That had also been her uncle's way, and one of her chosen tasks had been to sort and put volumes away when the chamber finally became too disordered. There was no guessing where to find what she wanted, and she dared not ask Sir Philip.

Dame Perpetua had already drifted away, opening aumbry doors and drawing volumes from the shelves, murmuring like a mother to beloved children as she went. This was a feast for her after the nine books that were all the priory had to offer. Given enough time, Dame Perpetua would gladly go through every book in the room. Somewhere among them were books of health, medicine, physic, surgery even, that might have what they sought. The problem was Sir Philip. He would have to be diverted, so they, or at least Dame Perpetua, could search unbothered.

Taking a book at random from the shelf beside them, she asked him, "You're a lover of books, too?"

"I doubt his worship the bishop would have recommended me to Master Chaucer if I were not."

Frevisse looked suitably impressed. "My uncle mentioned he had a new priest for the manor but said nothing in particular about you. Have you been here long?"

"Three years. Your uncle was a pleasant man to serve."

"But challenging upon occasion." Casually, Frevisse moved away from the shelves. "He enjoyed ideas, and discussing them with other knowledgeable people."

Sir Philip moved with her. "That's true enough. I had to make good use of his library here to keep even near to pace with him." He smiled at the memory; it was the warmest expression Frevisse had yet seen on him. "He was not given to quiet acceptance of anything."

"He had questions about most things, and wanted answers," Frevisse agreed.

"'To know wisdom and discipline, to understand the words of prudence, and to undertake the formation of doctrine, righteousness, fate, and . . .'" Sir Philip hesitated over what came next.

"'. . . equity,'" Frevisse supplied, "'that subtlety be given to little children, and to those waxing in years, cunning and understanding.' From the first chapter of Proverbs." Caught up again in the game she had so often played with Chaucer, one of them citing an authority, to see if the other could identify the source and, even better, complete the quotation. Without considering the propriety of saying so in such company, she said, "So the wise collect proverbs, saith Solomon. But my uncle and I—and you, I think?—would collect whole books instead."

Sir Philip nodded. "You're quite right, and widely read, I gather. All the books in Master Chaucer's library?"

"All the ones that he had when I lived here. But so many of these I've never seen. No one seems to feel books would be a benefit to the nunnery, though 'Saint Paul says that all that is written is written to our learning—'" Deliberately she stopped short of the quotation's end.

"'So take the grain and let the chaff be still,'" Sir Philip said, gravely carrying it through. "That is from Geoffrey Chaucer's tales and 'Now, good God, if it be your will as says my lord, so make us all good men, and bring us to his high bliss, amen.'"

"Amen." Frevisse picked up a book lying on the window seat beside them and idly opened it. It was in Latin verse, and scanning a few lines, she recognized it for Ovid. Her uncle and—he had said—his father had both loved Ovid's work. She had occasionally regretted her own Latin was too weak to share their pleasure in it. She closed the book and laid it down again, wondering who had had it out. Sir Philip? Carefully, beginning to want to know more about him, she said, "My uncle was forever asking his priest to find out at length about one thing or another. Had he asked you for something in particular in the while you've been here?"

"Lately he had me copying various books he wanted for his own. I finished a new work of Boccaccio's at Michaelmas—"

"New?" Frevisse asked ironically. The Italian writer had died well back in the last century.

"Newly in English at any rate." The corners of his mouth twitched. If Frevisse had thought him given to amusement, she would have suspected he was suppressing a smile. He said, "It's a very traditional tirade against women. Quite passionate actually."

Aware that he was watching for her reaction while he spoke, Frevisse asked with unfeigned amusement, "Did he do a matching treatise equally fair to men?"

Sir Philip laughed aloud, deep and full and so surprising

that Dame Perpetua looked up from the book she held and
Master Lionel broke his concentration on a handful of
papers long enough to stare offended at them before
returning to his work.

"The translator assures us," Sir Philip said, "that the work
is put into English for its literary form, not its sentiments."

"How very comforting," Frevisse responded drily. "How
did my uncle come by it?"

"He borrowed it from his grace the duke of Gloucester
with permission to make copy of it—"

"The duke of Gloucester? The duke of Gloucester loaned
one of his precious books to a relative of Bishop *Beaufort*?"

Besides creating scandals and upheaval in the royal
government, principally against Bishop Beaufort, the king's
uncle Gloucester's great passion was a devoted—and
expensive—pursuit of books not readily had in England.

"A precious book of which I daresay the duke's and your
uncle's may be presently the only copies. His grace of
Gloucester commissioned the translation. It seems the love
of books is stronger than the hatreds of politics."

"It must be." But then her uncle had never been particularly good at hatreds. "They take too much energy and
concentration," he had said. "I have better things to do."

Sir Philip looked across the room toward the desks beside
the window. He hesitated, then said, "Lately Master Chaucer
had set me to copying out a book of the deeds of Arthur that
I'd never seen before. Or to be more precise, the deeds of Sir
Gawain. Would you care to see it?"

"Yes! Assuredly!"

"It's here." Sir Philip crossed to the smaller desk, behind
Chaucer's but placed the same way, left end to the window
for better light for the writer's work. Frevisse followed him
as he folded back the cloth covering the desk's slanted top

to reveal a sheet written half-over in fine, black italic script next to a thin book held open by a copyist's usual small lead bars laid across the top of its pages. With care that told how much he valued the book, Sir Philip put aside the bars and inserted a paper scrap in his place before picking it up and handing it to her.

It was bound in green leather, soft to her touch. Frevisse stroked it, delaying the pleasure of opening a work she did not know. But only briefly; her eagerness was too much.

"It's in English," she said in surprise. Most stories of King Arthur that she had encountered were in French. Not all, but most.

"And verse, for good measure," Sir Philip said.

"'Since the siege and the assault was ceased at Troy,
    The burgh broken and burned to brands and ashes,
    The man that the trammels of treason there
    wrought . . .'"

Frevisse read. "Oh, this has a goodly way to it!" Forgetful of any other purpose, she sank down on the window seat, intent on the wonder of having something entirely new to read. "'If you'll listen this lay but a little while . . .'"

"Here's where you've all gone to!"

Startled, Frevisse looked up, along with Dame Perpetua. Sir Philip turned sharply. Only Master Lionel kept on with his business; no one ever came looking for him. One of Aunt Matilda's maidservants entered the room. "Can you come?" she asked with a quick curtsy directed at both Frevisse and Sir Philip. "My lady the countess prays it. My lady her mother has taken to crying again and can't stop. My lady the countess feels one or the other or both of you might be able to help her."

Frevisse was already rising and putting the book back on the desk as Sir Philip said, "Assuredly."

"Dame Perpetua, will you stay here?" Frevisse asked. There would be no fear of impropriety in Master Lionel's presence, and this was the chance they needed.

"If I may," Dame Perpetua said. She had made no move to relinquish the book she was holding. "I doubt I'd serve more than small purpose in going."

Frevisse nodded briskly and followed Sir Philip and the maidservant out of the room.

Chapter
🔹 13 🔹

WHEN FREVISSE CAME into her aunt's bedchamber she found Matilda lying in bed desperately clinging to Alice's hands and Alice saying soothing things in a voice that told she had been saying them for a long while. Matilda's face was ravaged with tears and hopeless crying. Frevisse went to her and laid a hand on her shaking shoulder under the covers. Still holding with one hand to Alice, Aunt Matilda reached the other to grasp Frevisse's wrist, sobbing brokenly, "I miss him so much! I miss him so much!"

"I know, Aunt. I know. I do, too," Frevisse said with aching sincerity, and without warning was crying with her, huge, unbearable tears scalding down her cheeks.

Sir Philip joined her at the bedside. His voice warmer than Frevisse had ever heard it, and calm with deep authority, he said, "My dear lady, you've made yourself ill with your grieving. You'll break your heart if you go on, and think what your husband would say to see you like this."

Matilda choked on a sob and with the ghost of a smile trembling on her lips, said, "He . . . he would say . . . 'N-now, Maud. Now, Maud.'"

"Exactly so. So imagine he's saying that to you and try to

find the peace he would want you to have." He bent over her, not to give blessing but to tuck the embroidered cover more comfortably under her chin. "You're over-wearied and must stay in bed all this day. You've been too brave for too long and need your rest to regain your strength, just as Master Chaucer would want you to. If you want anything, we'll joyfully do or bring it." He glanced around the room, eliciting a nod or faint murmur of agreement from everyone there. "You see? We love you, too, and want you well again. We've lost the head of our household; we could not bear to lose its heart."

Aunt Matilda sniffed tremulously and managed a watery smile. Tears still stood in her eyes but the raw edge of hysteria was gone. She had let go of Frevisse's hand and was holding Sir Philip's now.

He turned to one of the women holding a goblet at the foot of the bed. "Is that for my lady?"

"A sleeping potion, sir."

She held it out and he took it. Alice lifted her mother on the pillows, and, still holding her hand, Sir Philip gently held the goblet to Matilda's lips, waiting patiently while she drank it a sip at a time, until she had taken it all. Then he handed the goblet away and took her hand in both of his.

"You'll stay with me?" she quavered. "Even while I sleep? You'll stay with me and pray? For Thomas?"

"And for you, my lady. I'll be here when you awaken," he promised.

Worn-out, she did not resist whatever had been in the drink but soon slipped into a drowse, with tears still on her cheeks. Even with the drug, it was a shallow sleep, pathetic in its fragility.

Frevisse had drawn back from the bed while Sir Philip tended to her aunt. Now, with everyone keeping very still for fear of disturbing the sleeper, and Sir Philip clearly intending to stay there for as long as he had promised, she slipped sideways to the door and out. Silently, she edged the door closed but not latched behind her, whispered, "She sleeps, but only lightly," to the pair of serving maids hovering in the outer chamber, and gave them no time to ask her anything else, but went briskly on.

Now, while for this once she could be sure of where he was, she meant to look through Sir Philip's room.

If she had met anyone in the chapel's antechamber, she would have simply gone in, as if intent on prayers. But there was no one, and she went up the narrow stairs in soft-footed haste. Outside his door she paused to rap sharply, lest his servant be there. No one called out, and she went in.

The bed had been made, the shutters set open to the pallid sunlight. The sparsely furnished room was neatened to the point of being utterly impersonal. There was no trace of the chaos of emotion and desperation yesterday.

Frevisse crossed to the table. She touched her fingertips to its scrubbed top, where Sir Clement had fallen forward, as if an answer might come to her by that. Nothing did. She looked around and saw the only closed place was the aumbry, from where the bottle and goblet that had given Sir Clement his last drink had come. She opened its doors to three neatly ordered shelves. The bottle on the bottom one, beside two cups and a pewter plate was not yesterday's; this one's cork had not been pulled. She took up the nearest cup and found it unremarkable, of blue-glazed pottery, simple, undecorated, austere like the rest of the room. Its fellow matched it. The plate might have come from a peasant's cottage.

On the middle shelf was a golden casket. Even before she opened it, Frevisse knew that it must contain the essentials for the last sacrament. She crossed herself, took it down, and reverently opened it. Everything appeared exactly as it ought to, with the tiny jars of chrism and holy water, a gilt crucifix, a small wax candle, and a pyx. She closed the box and rubbed her fingers with her thumb, to remove any trace of holy particles.

Feeling guilty for her intrusiveness, she reached among and behind the few pieces of folded clothing on the upper shelf for anything hastily put out of sight and found nothing.

She went to the bed. The straw-filled mattress rustled at her prodding. She stooped to look underneath. There were only the ropes laced through a plain wooden frame and his servant's more narrow truckle bed. Careful even in her haste, she felt all through the coverings of Sir Philip's bed and then pulled out the servant's and did the same. Finding nothing, she unmade them, to inspect the mattresses. Neither showed any sign of having been cut open and sewn shut again and, hoping she did it identically to how they had been, she remade both beds.

She tried the prie-dieu next, running her hands along its sides and tilting the bench to look at its underside. As nearly as she could tell, there was nowhere for a hidden place in it. The cushion on the kneeler was firmly tacked down along all its edges and though she kneaded the cushion thoroughly with both hands she could detect nothing odd about its stuffing.

The desk remained. Like the prie-dieu it seemed to have no secret places, and the books were commonplace ones. A worn psalter, an *Oculus Sacerdotis* with a carved leather cover, the ubiquitous *Lay Folks Catechism*, from which Frevisse and nearly everyone she knew had been taught their prayers in childhood, and a handsome copy of *Stimulus Amoris*, written to stir the reader's love of God. Frevisse riffled through the pages of each one, finding the first three to be plain copies of indifferent craftsmanship, heavily annotated in all their margins in firm, dark writing. The *Stimulus Amoris* was another matter. Its script had been done in a clear, steady hand meant to make the words as lovely in their seeming as in their meaning; what notes there were, were lightly done, as if to distract from the beauty of the pages as little as might be. And it was illuminated as the other books were not, painted throughout with pictures in bright, exquisite detail, shining among the pages. Despite where she was, and why, Frevisse lingered over the book.

When she put it back at last and looked around the room, she could find nothing else to question. There was nothing here to suggest murder.

But why should there be? Sir Philip had had all night to dispose of anything dangerous to himself. A trip to the necessarium, a bottle, a packet, a screw of paper dropped down the hole, and he was rid of evidence that he had killed a man. But aside from that, it was difficult to imagine that he had had some sort of poison in his room at all. Why would he? On the chance he might someday have occasion, desire, or chance to use it? If he were indeed a man who kept poison to hand that purposefully, he was far different and more dangerous than he seemed.

Or had he had poison to hand especially for Sir Clement? Knowing for weeks that Chaucer would die, and that almost surely Sir Clement would come to the funeral, had he prepared for the chance? But then how had he given him the poison at the feast and again in the room? For surely it had to have been a double dose of the same poison for the symptoms to be the same?

She had the *why* Sir Philip might have done it: Sir Clement was a threat to his advancement in the Church. But the *how* eluded her. In the room, yes, there might have been chance, but in the hall Sir Philip had been seated far down the table from Sir Clement and not come near him until after Sir Clement had been stricken.

Wait. Yes, he had.

He had gone to Sir Clement on the occasion of Sir Clement's outburst, had spoken with him. Had there been chance then to put something in his food? Frevisse shut her eyes, trying to remember the scene. He had come up behind Sir Clement, but she could not recall that he had ever bent over the table or even come close to it. Dishes and drink had been well out of his easy reach; anything he might have done that way would have been obvious to someone.

Then had he had help? An accomplice from among other victims of Sir Clement's tormenting, willing to share the risk and not likely to become a greater threat to Sir Philip than Sir Clement was? Who had been in a position to do what needed to be done at the table in the hall?

Jevan, of course, with access to every dish he had served to his uncle there. He could have easily introduced poison to some dish before serving it. And Guy and Lady Anne had both been there, in reach of the dishes after they were served. It had been Guy who took the bottle and cup from the aumbry here in Sir Philip's room, before Sir Clement's final attack. Had they planned that far ahead, to have poison to hand here if Sir Clement failed to die in the hall?

It would surely have been best if he had died at the table, saving the peril of giving him more poison. That brought her back to the continuing question of how he could have been poisoned there and no one else affected. Unless . . . she had read somewhere that a poison taken in small doses long enough would be rendered harmless to the person taking it.

That was too complicated. Surely that was too complicated, involving too many people—Sir Philip, Guy, Anne, possibly Jevan—over too long a time. Unless she could find they were acquainted before now and had been in contact with each other months ago.

Frevisse realized she had lingered a dangerously long time in a room where she had no right to be. Belatedly she realized there was one last place to look, and brought the stool from the table to stand on so she could see the aumbry's top. Nothing was there, not even an appreciable accumulation of dust; Sir Philip's servant was thorough at his work.

Careful to replace the stool exactly, she went to open the door enough to look out. There was no one there, and she slipped out and down the stairs, still thinking. It would be simplest if God had indeed struck Sir Clement in the hall, meaning to give an awful but not fatal warning, and then a human hand had taken advantage of the moment to poison him in Sir Philip's room. Only Guy and Sir Philip had handled the cup of wine. Guy had opened the bottle—and by its cork it had been opened before. Had there been chance for someone else to put something into the cup as it went from the aumbry to Sir Clement's hand? She had not been watching. She did not remember. It was possible, though it would have been far easier to have put the poison in the bottle beforehand. And it needn't have been Sir Philip, though it was his bottle and his chamber. Anyone might have chosen his—or her—time and come in to do that, just as Frevisse had chosen hers. Though that carried the risk of someone other than Sir Clement being poisoned.

Who was desperate enough to do any of this?

Sir Philip, who might have had no better chance to be rid of Sir Clement's threat. Lady Anne, who was in love with Guy but threatened with marriage to Sir Clement whom she openly detested, according to Robert. Guy, Sir Clement's heir, wanting Lady Anne for himself, hating his uncle. Jevan Dey, tired of Sir Clement's insults and torments.

They had all been there. And the physician, but he at least had no reason to want Sir Clement dead. Or no reason that Frevisse knew of, she amended.

She had reached the bottom of the stairs and was crossing the antechamber to return to her aunt when the chapel door began to open behind her. Instantly, because it was easier than having someone wonder why she had been up to Sir Philip's room, Frevisse swung around, to seem that she was just coming toward the chapel.

Lady Anne, coming out, bent her head in slight, silent greeting, and would have gone past except Frevisse said, "Please accept my sympathy on Sir Clement's death."

The girl's face had been quiet, her summer-blue eyes down after her glance at Frevisse. Now she looked up, a corner of her cupid mouth slightly awry, as if something amused her that she knew should not. "Thank you."

Frevisse asked, "Is Sir Philip in the chapel?"

"Sir Philip?" Lady Anne's puzzlement was clear. "Who . . . ?"

"The priest who was with Sir Clement at . . . the end, yesterday." Frevisse dropped her voice and eyes as if not wishing to intrude on or add to Lady Anne's grief.

"Oh. I didn't know his name. No, I haven't seen him today."

She walked on. Frevisse went with her, asking with seeming casualness, "Will you be leaving soon, as soon as . . ." She paused over the words, delicately short of mentioning matters that might be distressing to the girl.

With no apparent distress, Lady Anne said, "As soon as the crowner says we may, yes."

"And you'll take Sir Clement's body with you?"

"Oh, no. Some of our people will follow after with it. With the cold, we'll ride on as fast as may be."

Frevisse said in a discreet tone, slightly changing the subject, "He wasn't a well-liked man, was he?"

"He was a hated man," Lady Anne said without qualm. "By a great many people."

"And now you'll be free to marry Guy, won't you?"

Lady Anne stopped to look at her wide-eyed. "How do you know that?"

Frevisse made a light gesture. "People gossip and I can't always help hearing them." More to see Lady Anne's response than because it was her own opinion, she added, "He seems a goodly young man."

Lady Anne's smile brightened her eyes to dazzling. "He is! Oh, indeed he is!" A little mischievously, she asked, "Did the gossips also know we're to be married as soon as the banns have been cried?"

"They didn't know that, no." Frevisse found the girl's smile infectious, and was glad Lady Anne's slender body precluded suspicion that desperate need more than desire was behind her eagerness to marry.

But such great love, long thwarted by Sir Clement as it had been, could have grown desperate for that reason alone. Was Guy's desire for her as great as hers for him?

But Lady Anne was going on about his virtues with all the certainty of youth that they would be enough to bring them happiness. "He's handsome. Anyone can see that. And brave. You should see him on the tourney field. And Sir Clement's heir. He'll have everything now that Sir Clement is dead. I think that's why Sir Clement hated him. Sir Clement never wanted anyone to have anything of his. How disappointed he must be to find himself dead and everything gone into Guy's hands." She was clearly delighted with the idea.

"I actually heard him call Guy murderous during that quarrel in the great hall."

"He was always saying things like that! Miserable man."

"But Guy never fought him over it?"

Lady Anne's pretty face tightened into an expression of deep disgust. "He never would. He said he owed Sir Clement duty as head of the family. But that whole business of him trying to murder Sir Clement always made me so *angry*."

"Guy tried to *murder* him?"

"No, of course not." Lady Anne laughed. "Sometime before I was his ward, for Christmas or Michaelmas or Lady Day or some such, Guy brought him marchpane for a gift. Sir Clement had a greedy tooth for sweets and should have been well-pleased. Rude, as always, of course, but pleased. Instead he raged that Guy was trying to poison him and even threw the marchpane—all of it—on the floor!" The waste of so much sugar, butter, almonds, and whatever else delicious might have been in the expensive treat clearly appalled her.

"Why? Did the marchpane make him ill?"

"He didn't even taste it! He just looked at it and threw it down! Afterwards he was forever calling Guy a murderous whelp or something like, but Guy never heeded and neither did anyone else. Everyone knew what Sir Clement was like."

"Then it was very good of you to have been in the chapel praying for him."

Lady Anne made the expression of amused exasperation used by women indulging the man they love. "Guy says it will be best to show what courtesy we can toward him, now that we won't have to do it much longer. But I doubt prayers will do Sir Clement any good, do you? I think he went straight to hell and there's the end of it." They had reached the door to the series of rooms the women guests had shared; by now Lady Anne and her women would be nearly the only ones left. Lady Anne, letting Frevisse see she was ready to be done with her company, made her a pretty little curtsy and said, "If you will excuse me, Dame."

Frevisse bent her head in acceptance and farewell, but before she could go her own way, Guy came from the room as if in haste to somewhere else.

"Guy!" Lady Anne exclaimed, moving eagerly toward him and holding out her hands to him.

He caught and kissed them, right and left. "I came to see if you were back from prayers yet and you weren't. Are you all right?"

Lady Anne made a face of distaste. "I've prayed all I can stomach for him and I'm not doing any more. You didn't come. You said you would."

"I said I might. I've been seeing to what can be done so we can leave as soon as the crowner finishes with us."

"Has he come yet?"

"Not yet, but soon, I should think."

"He shouldn't even be needed. Everyone saw what happened. It was an act of God. The bishop's word alone should be enough for it. Shouldn't it?" she appealed to Frevisse.

"You would think so, but the law has its own way about these things." To Guy she added, "Lady Anne and I have been talking of your uncle."

"My cousin," Guy corrected politely. "Or rather my father's cousin and so mine once removed."

"And the farther removed the better," Lady Anne said.

She was holding on to Guy's arm now, ready to go away with him, but Frevisse continued her relentless gossiping. "Lady Anne was telling me how he's kept a quarrel with you these many years."

"Oh, yes." Guy smiled with rueful good humor. "The infamous marchpane."

Jevan appeared behind him. "My lord," he said.

Guy looked over his shoulder—toward but not directly at him—and said curtly, "Yes?"

"There's a question of what can be packed and what you'll want while you're still here."

"You can't decide?"

"It would be better if you did."

"I'll see to it," Lady Anne said. "I have to ask my maid about something anyway."

She kissed Guy's cheek lightly. Beyond Guy, Frevisse saw Jevan's face was bleak with a control that did not quite hold before he stepped back with a bow to let Lady Anne go past him.

Frevisse remembered something she had wanted to ask and said brightly, "Oh, Lady Anne—and you gentlemen, too—I was wondering . . . Master Broun who was with Sir Clement at his death—God keep his soul—Master Broun was saying he saw the mark of a hand on Sir Clement's face." She lowered her voice impressively, much as the physician had done. "A red mark as if an inhumanly large hand had slapped him. I had to admit I didn't see it, but I was wondering if you had? It would be such a great wonder."

Lady Anne said after a moment's hesitation, "Why, no, I never saw anything like that."

"Nor I," Jevan agreed.

"He was just all welts all over," Guy said. "Maybe it was

on his other cheek than the one I saw," he added helpfully.

"No, I saw both sides of his face," Jevan said. "There were only the welts, no pattern to them."

"Oh. That's that then," Guy said, and added, "Go on with Lady Anne."

Jevan bowed, and as he followed Lady Anne away, Frevisse asked Guy, "You'll keep him in your service?"

Guy shrugged. "For a time anyway. He's knowledgeable about Sir Clement's affairs so he'll be useful awhile."

"And then?"

"He was Sir Clement's dog. I'll be rid of him as soon as may be. He can find employment elsewhere."

"But he didn't like Sir Clement any better than you did."

"He served him nonetheless. And he has too much of his look. I don't want him around me."

"Did Sir Clement make provision for him, or will he have nothing when you let him go?"

The impertinence of her questions had begun to penetrate his absorption with his own affairs. Frowning, he said, "I've no idea." And added, "If you'll excuse me, my lady."

Chapter

14

VERY FEW OF the other guests were to be inconvenienced by the crowner's coming. Only those who had been nearest Sir Clement at the feast supposed they had to stay, but they were precisely the people Frevisse wanted to talk with, and since the morning was worn away well toward ten o'clock and dinnertime, she guessed they could be found in the hall, a warm and convenient gathering place.

They were there, a lady and five men, three of them booted and cloaked for travel, standing at one end of the dais, out of the way since the servants were busy setting up the tables only in the lower part of the hall, in token that the family would not be dining here this midday. With a touch of dismay, Frevisse realized she did not know any of them by name, but as a member of the family she had reason to approach them, to ask after their well-being, and join politely in their conversation. She and the lady exchanged slight curtsies; the men removed their hats and bowed to her; she bent her head to them. Their talk had broken off at her coming. To set it going again she said, "I hope you've been made comfortable. If there's anything you need . . ." Her gesture indicated it was theirs to ask for.

"We're doing very well, thank you, my dear," the lady said. She was middle-aged, wide, and comfortably matter-of-fact. "How does poor Matilda?"

"Very poorly at present, I fear. It's all been too much for her, with Uncle Thomas's death and then that dreadful trouble at the feast."

"Bad business," one of the cloaked men said, shaking his head. "Bad business all around. Not a good way to go, and a pity it had to happen here."

"It was bound to happen somewhere. He'd asked for it over and over," one of the others said. He gave a knowing wink. "Is there any of us who haven't heard him bluster for God's judgment a score of times at the least?"

"I thought he'd done it less often of late," said one of the men not dressed for travel. "The times I've been with him this past year or so, he seemed less given to it."

"Not that you spent any more time in his company than you could help! St. Roche, but that man was a plague to everyone around him." The cloaked man shook his head with a bitter grin of remembrance, then bethought himself and added, "God keep his soul."

"The devil more likely. But there's no denying his sheep had some of the best wool this part of Oxfordshire."

"That's young Jevan's doing, not old Clement's. Old Clement wasted his brains in looking for quarrels, but that youngling knows what he's about with sheep."

The talk veered off to wool and overseas prices, confirming Frevisse's thought that the men ready to leave were likely merchants. The other two, because they had sat at the table near Sir Clement, must be knights, and one of them did not join in the general talk but stood gravely a little behind the lady who, though probably his wife, was taking knowledgeable part in the wool talk. Frevisse eased toward him and said aside from the flow of the conversation, "You were seated near to Sir Clement at the feast, I think?"

The man was tall, with a soft voice. "I had that misfortune, yes. Next to the young lady."

"Sir Clement quarreled with you during the feast, didn't he?"

"Over a matter of grazing rights that was settled in court three years ago, but since legality never mattered to him, he brought it up whenever we had the misfortune to meet. Like Jack says"—he nodded at the merchant who had claimed to see a mellowing in Sir Clement of late—"he'd lost some of his edge at making new quarrels, but he could still hold to his old ones well enough."

"So he hadn't truly changed his ways?"

The man gave a faint, mild smile. "He'd maybe worn out his fondness for saying 'May God strike me down' so often, but he could still make life a hell for anyone in his reach."

"Still, Ralph, he'd given up fisting anyone in the face who displeased him," put in the other knight. He had sat next to Guy at the feast, Frevisse suddenly remembered. "I'd noticed that of late."

"Ah, that's because he was growing too old for it, Sir Edward," Sir Ralph's lady said.

"Maybe it finally came to him that someone would fist him back someday if he went on the way he was," the shorter and rounder of the merchants said.

"Someone should have, and a long time ago."

There were noddings and general agreement. They were plainly enjoying the chance to cut at Sir Clement now that it was safe to do so.

"He made that poor girl's life none too easy," Sir Ralph's lady said. Then she added mostly under her breath, "And now she'll do the same for Guy, I'd guess." She and

Frevisse exchanged private smiles, understanding that dainty Lady Anne had a will of her own.

The men began talking of Guy's good fortune. Now that Sir Clement was out of his way, he was expected to do well.

"He's a solid enough fellow, with none of the crotchets that family seems to carry like other folks pass on brown hair," the short merchant said. "But the day isn't going to better for our staying here and we ought to be on our way. We only stayed to talk with you this while longer, and now we have."

He embraced the lady, dropped a casual kiss in the vicinity of her cheek, and said, "You take care, Eleanor. No rheums this year, you hear?"

"And the same to you, brother," she returned. "We'll expect you at Christmas if you know what's good for you."

There were handshakes and bows all around, and the three merchants left the hall in a bustle of cloaks and servants.

"Ah, now, I'll miss him," Lady Eleanor said wistfully.

Her husband took her by the arm and drew her close. "Christmas isn't so far off," he said comfortingly.

"If the weather doesn't have us all pent-up like badgers by then," Sir Edward said. "All the signs say this will be a bitter year."

"It's been bitter enough for Sir Clement already," Frevisse said. The three of them would leave to sit to dinner soon, and there were still things she wanted to ask them before then, so she returned directly to Sir Clement. "I'll be asked so many questions when I return to St. Frideswide's, but I was so far away from what happened. You were all beside him at the feast. What especially did you see?"

The three looked at each other. Sir Edward shrugged as if he could think of nothing special, and Lady Eleanor answered more fully, "Why, nothing in particular. Si

Clement was simply being offensive, as always, and I faced away from him as much as might be, talking to the lady on my other side. Until he quarreled with my lord." She smiled sympathetically up at her husband. "And not very long after that he began to make strange sounds. *That* was terrifying, let me tell you!"

"I thought he'd choked on something at first," Sir Ralph said.

"There wasn't any warning? He just began to choke?" Frevisse asked. She did not know what she was trying to learn, but if she kept asking questions, someone might say something that mattered.

Sir Ralph shook his head. "After his outburst at me—and mine at him, I lost some of my temper, too," he admitted to his wife's knowing prod at his ribs, "we all set to eating again. He snapped at a server for not refilling his wine fast enough, but that was all."

"Jevan was waiting on him then?"

"Not with the wine," Sir Edward said. "That was all from the household servers, moving in front of the tables, you know, and keeping an eye on everyone. They did well. Your aunt's to be complimented on her people."

"But lightning itself wouldn't move fast enough for Sir Clement," Lady Eleanor said.

They agreed on that, and went on chatting until dinner was called. Then Frevisse assured them her aunt was most sorry for the inconvenience to them, and received their assurances that they held no one responsible for the trouble—except Sir Clement who continued to be a trial even in death, they agreed—and they all parted in mutual goodwill.

Dame Perpetua was still in Chaucer's library, huddled down on a stool in front of one of the aumbries with an open book on her lap, too intent on it to notice Frevisse's arrival. Across the room Master Lionel, scrutinizing a selection of documents laid out along the window seat, did not acknowledge her, either. Amused, Frevisse slipped across the room to lay a hand on Dame Perpetua's shoulder.

The other nun twitched her head a little and said, "Mmmm?" without looking up.

"Is it a good book?" Frevisse asked.

"Mmmm." Dame Perpetua drew her attention reluctantly away to blink up at her, decided she was really there, and said enthusiastically, "It's *Mandeville's Travels*! I haven't read it since I was a girl. I loved it. All those wonders—"

Knowing how long Dame Perpetua could go on about a book, Frevisse interrupted, "Did you find anything useful to our problem?"

Dame Perpetua's face blanked, then she brightened. "Indeed I did! Here." She set Mandeville aside and took up one of the volumes lying beside her. "Your uncle was wonderful. There are books here about everything. I could stay forever. This one is a *Materia Medica*, with a whole part just about poisons and their effects."

Frevisse took it. "How did you manage to find it? And so quickly?"

"I asked Master Lionel," Dame Perpetua said with the simplicity of the obvious. She lowered her voice. "He doesn't want to talk to anyone, but he knows where everything is. I asked about poisons, and he showed me this one right away."

"Does it have what we need?"

Dame Perpetua looked abashed. "I decided to let you see for yourself if it's any help, while I . . ." She lovingly touched the book in her lap.

Frevisse knew she had been no better herself with the

Gawain book earlier that morning. She smiled and said, "Then I'll look into it. You go on."

The book was everything Dame Perpetua had said it was. A little skimming of the pages brought her to the part about poisons, just after a treatise on the diagnosing of humors according to the planets. She sat on the chair at Sir Philip's desk, laid open the book, and began to read. Her Latin was imperfect, but unlike literature, this was mostly straightforward text and she could follow its gist, translating the fragments that were pertinent to the question. Was there a poison whose symptoms matched Sir Clement's fatal ones?

The list ranged from commonly known poisons found in any English woodland or roadside to exotic ones difficult to obtain except from very specialized merchants with the most exotic of contacts. It seemed very complete.

And none of the poisons listed created symptoms that matched Sir Clement's.

There were ones signified by difficulty in breathing but not the swollen, strangled closing of the throat Dr. Broun had described. There were vomitings of different quality and color, and sometimes fits or mania, but Sir Clement had been quite clear in his mind and not given any sign of being even sick to his stomach, let alone vomiting. As for discolorations of the body, particularly of extremities, there were no suggestions of his general blotching of itching welts on face and arms.

If Sir Clement had been poisoned, it was not with any poison described in what seemed to be a most scrupulously thorough book.

Dame Perpetua had been paying closer heed than Frevisse had thought. She said from across the room, "It doesn't have what you want?"

"No."

"Then perhaps Bishop Beaufort is wrong. Perhaps it was God's hand against Sir Clement."

"No."

Dame Perpetua made no effort to hide her surprise. "You don't think so anymore?"

"I'm not *sure* anymore. Not the way we were sure when it happened. I want to ask more questions. Will you look for another book on poisons? There might well be another."

"If you think it's needed, certainly." Dame Perpetua put down the Mandeville.

Frevisse had noted that Master Lionel, ceasing to shuffle among his papers while she talked, had been standing still with his head partly turned to listen. Now she said directly to him, "Will you help Dame Perpetua with this, Master Lionel?"

The old clerk's head snapped away and his hands began to move busily among his papers. But he made a sound that might have been agreement, and Dame Perpetua smiled and nodded in confirmation.

Satisfied that between them they would do far more than she could, Frevisse left them to it.

Frevisse went to Aunt Matilda's chamber. Her aunt lay sleeping, her plump body under the covers, her slackened, ravaged face looking vulnerable. Her daughter had sent for her sewing and was sitting comfortably on a cushion under the window, coloring a rose pink with silk thread. She looked up when Frevisse entered and put a long finger in front of her pursed lips. Frevisse nodded and went to peer more closely at her aunt, who never stirred. Joan was sitting on a stool beside the bed, staring at her mistress, her own face wretched.

Frevisse bowed her head and offered a prayer for the solace of this sad company, and left.

The kitchen of Ewelme manor house was large, floored with stone flags, and rising two stories to a roof set with louvers that could be opened to let the smoke and heat out. A tray of roasted chickens was cooling on a table, and a cook's helper was leaning gingerly into a low-burning fireplace to stir a large pot hanging over the coals. The cook himself was seated on a tall stool, wiping his strong-looking hands with a clean towel. When he saw Frevisse, he rose at once to his feet and bowed twice.

"You grace this room with your presence," he said, bowing yet again. He spoke with an accent Frevisse could not identify. He was a tall man, with dark, curly hair that glistened as if washed in oil, and he moved his hands eloquently as he spoke. "Is there some way I may help you? Something I may bring to you?"

"Will you answer one or two questions?" returned Frevisse.

"Of course, if I can. Do you want a recipe to take back with you to your nunnery?" He turned to the helper. "I require a bit of paper, a quill, and some ink, at once!"

But Frevisse raised a hand to stop the helper. "No, it is nothing like that. This concerns the funeral feast, from which a guest had to be helped, who later died."

The cook sat down as if someone had cut his hamstrings. But he said nothing, only waited.

"Do you know the man who died? Sir Clement?"

"No, madam. But he sent his servant in to speak to me about the menu for the feast."

"Which servant?"

"I do not know, madam. A lean fellow, with brown hair and a sad face."

"Why was Sir Clement interested in the menu?"

"Because, I gather, he had an unhappy stomach, which required certain things to keep its balance."

"What things?"

The cook gave a lengthy sigh, held up a hand, and began to count on his fingers. "The milk used in the making of any dish must be fresh, as Sir Clement could not abide sour milk; his saltcellar must be full and clean, as he used a good deal of salt on his food, and was inclined to throw a contaminated saltcellar on the floor; any dish containing nuts must be announced when it was brought to his place, as he would not, under any circumstances, eat anything containing nuts; and the goblet he drank from must be silver or gold as he could not bear the taste pewter gave to his drink. I will say what I told this servant, madam, that I assured Sir Clement's servant that only the finest, freshest, and most costly ingredients were going into every dish prepared in this house, and that the final remove, which Sir Clement never got a chance to throw on the floor, contained filberts. And I had the impertinence to ask if Sir Clement had brought a goblet of his own to use, as it was quite impossible for us to take a goblet reserved for, say, the duke of Norfolk and give it to Sir Clement's use. And it transpired he had, as this problem had arisen before on Sir Clement's journeying, and he had learned to bring his own." The cook had set off on this story calmly, had become indignant by the middle of it, but cooled to triumphant amusement by the end. The cook's helper, by his expression, stood ready to back the cook in every particular, so Frevisse did not question him, only asked the cook to make a copy of the feast menu, which he did. She tucked it up her sleeve, thanked him for his cooperation, and withdrew.

She decided to go see if Master Lionel had performed another prompt, masterly trick with the book search. But to her surprise Dame Perpetua was not in Chaucer's chamber. Frevisse paused in the doorway, looking around to be sure she was not crouched behind the desk or a stack of books. Someone had lighted a fire in the small fireplace against the day's deepening cold; its bright flickering against the gray light falling through the windows made a slight promise of warmth, but Master Lionel was busy at his chest half the room away from it, oblivious both to its possibilities and her entering. And Sir Philip was standing at the window, staring out with a troubled frown easy to read even across the room.

The frown smoothed itself away as easily as warmed wax slips down the side of a candle, and his voice was merely its familiar neutral as he spoke. "Dame Frevisse. You expected Dame Perpetua, obviously."

She could not bring herself to care she might be endangering her reputation by being alone with a virile man, however priestly, with only a madman for a witness. As a compromise, she left the door open a crack. She was tired from her efforts, from talking endlessly to people, from being in a once-familiar place that had become strange to her. And she was chilled. She went to sit on a stool in front of the fire. Putting her feet forward and holding her hands out to the warmth, she said, "Am I sickening for something or is the day suddenly colder?"

"The day is suddenly much colder." Sir Philip held the flat of his hand toward the glass in front of him without quite touching it. "You can feel it pouring in as if the window were open. I'll not be surprised if the moat is frozen by morning."

Frevisse gave a weary sigh. There was the long ride back to St. Frideswide's to be endured in a day or two, and she could not decide whether she preferred bitter cold and firm roads or warmer weather and endless mire.

His back still to her, Sir Philip asked, "Are you free to talk now about Bishop Beaufort's interest in you?"

"To obey the bishop's will, I have had to ask questions of so many people that I doubt it is any secret. He does not believe Sir Clement died by God's hand."

"He thought that from the very first."

"And because my uncle told him I had a subtle intelligence, he asked me to learn whether it were indeed a miracle or not."

Sir Philip swung from the window to stare at her. "And have you?"

"I am sure it wasn't God who killed him."

The priest took that with admirably contained surprise. "Then who?"

Frevisse shook her head. "That I haven't learned. Or exactly how they did it. But it was at least begun at the feast, and as nearly as I can tell, you didn't have the chance to do anything to him there. At least not directly."

Sir Philip's brows drew together as he began to gather fully what she had said. "You suspected me? On what possible grounds? Or were you just generally suspecting everyone?"

"I am suspecting anyone who had an enemy in Sir Clement. You are on the list. If Sir Clement made good his claim that you were born in villeinage, your chance to rise high in the Church could be destroyed. By coming here for a reason not connected with you, Sir Clement gave you an opportunity, perhaps, to act against him without the suspicion that might be raised if you went to him, or caused him to be summoned here. It was a chance to be rid of him that you'd not likely have again."

"But there was no need for me to attack him, to murder him. I took care years ago to be sure the needful documents were all in order. There was no question of his having any claim over me, no matter how much he prated of it. And I made sure anyone who inquired and needed to know the futility of his insolence did know of it. He was an annoyance, not a threat."

Frevisse believed him. It was the kind of thing a man of Sir Philip's intelligence would have done. "But you've never told Bishop Beaufort that?"

"It would have been somewhat presumptuous of me to offer the information without being asked."

"But you know he's interested in you."

"He suggested to Master Chaucer that I might be of service to him, and to me that I could profit by learning the ways of an important household. I accepted Master Chaucer's offer gratefully. For one thing it simply gave me my brother's company for this while."

"Your brother?" The one Robert had not been sure was alive or not.

"Gallard Basing, the household usher. You didn't know?"

"No one told me your surname was Basing."

"I suppose there was no reason to. And we look nothing alike." He bounced a little on the balls of his feet, and his smile, twisted as it was in the webbing of scars on his face, was nevertheless charming.

He came to sit on his heels on the other side of the hearth, rubbing his hands as he held them out to the flames. The gesture reminded Frevisse of something—someone—but the half-memory slipped away behind the realization that Gallard Basing had had free movement through the hall all through the feast, and probably access to the food before it was served. Was Gallard protected by the same documents that protected Sir Philip? Did Gallard even know about the documents? How much did the brothers love one another? Trust one another? Use one another?

Her silence had drawn on too long; Sir Philip looked around and up into her face. "You didn't come to talk to me. You came to seek refuge among your uncle's books, didn't you?"

"A comfort remembered from childhood, I fear."

He smiled. Again Frevisse was surprised at how that, and the warm depths of his eyes, negated the ruin of the rest of his face. Perhaps it was merely that he did it so rarely. "A comfort I shall be sorry to leave," he said, "if my lord of Suffolk decides he wants a different house-priest than me."

"Won't Aunt Matilda have a say in that?"

Sir Philip shrugged. "I think that as her grief settles into her more deeply, your aunt is going to give up most of her interest in running this house. Perhaps she will join you at St. Frideswide's. It is not unknown for a widow to take the veil."

Frevisse dropped her gaze to her lap. If she did, she would make an unhappy nun, for silence, humility, and obedience were not Aunt Matilda's strongest virtues. Anyway, Sir Philip was right, the full center and single mainstay of her life had been her husband.

"Of course, Countess Alice may provide her with grandchildren, and give her new interest in life," the priest said. "We can only wait and see."

To change to an easier subject, Frevisse said, "Did my uncle ever say to you what he planned for his books after his death?"

"I think the best he's willed to Bishop Beaufort. Most of the rest are for Suffolk, and the remainder will be sold." Sir Philip's gaze traveled across the aumbries. "Your uncle had a taste for the unusual and rare as well as the precious."

"He valued every book he had as a candle lit against the darkness, against the ignorance we all sink into if we know only our own minds."

"And we all, by our nature, seek beyond our earthly limitations for God, so it is necessary that a book be goodly, if it is to give good instruction." He said this as if it had significance beyond the obvious.

But Frevisse did not know what point he was moving toward. She said, "I agree that mere individual reason cannot find God alone except by the greatest difficulty. Unless God himself comes to enlighten it."

"He comes to whom he chooses. 'God who cannot be comprehended by any man's intellect or by any angel's, since we and they are all created beings.'"

Frevisse smiled. "The *Cloud of Unknowing*. Uncle loved that book. He said he had no hope or inclination toward the contemplative life, but the idea of it gave him pleasure. He also said the *Unknowing* reminded him that 'It will be asked of you how you have spent the time you have been given.'"

"And we often forget that we have but one goal on earth: to earn heaven. 'Him I desire, Him I seek—'"

"'Nothing but Him.'" Frevisse said the last of the quotation with him. It was an idea to which she had given over her heart when she was young. She and Sir Philip smiled with shared understanding of something more than merely precious.

Then he said, "Since you've admitted to thinking I might be a murderer, may I ask about something I've suspected of you?"

"If you like."

"Your uncle had a psalter and gospels that isn't here anymore. I've looked, Master Lionel has looked. It's nowhere in this room, and he was always very careful to keep it here."

Frevisse nearly smiled, but she only raised one eyebrow and said nothing. Sir Philip went on, "I rather think you know what I speak of. You came away from your first meeting with the bishop carrying a closely wrapped bundle about the size of the missing book. I think he gave it to you, perhaps on the instructions of your uncle." He lowered his voice and leaned forward. "It is a copy of the vernacular translation by John Wycliffe."

Over fifty years ago, John Wycliffe had presumed to translate the Bible into English, that all men might read and ponder freely on its words without the interpretation or control of the Church. Except that he had had powerful friends among the nobility, Wycliffe would have been condemned by the Church and burned as a heretic. As it was, he had died free and in his bed; not until 1417 had his bones been dug up, burned, and the ashes thrown into a river. But from the very first, his Englished Bible had been a forbidden thing, though copies turned up in some unlikely places, including nunneries. Chaucer had had the psalms and gospels kept in an obscure corner among other, unoffending books of theology, and there Frevisse had found it as a girl. She had delighted in being able to read freely what was so slow and difficult for her to follow in Latin. Chaucer had not forbidden it to her, and her faith had never been hurt by it, only her dependence on what any ignorant priest might choose to say the Bible said.

"Do you have it?" Sir Philip asked.

"I haven't seen it," she said with perfect truth. Then honesty compelled her to add, "But I haven't opened the package Bishop Beaufort gave to me."

Master Lionel straightened from a sheaf of documents he

held and stared down the room at her. His sudden focus on something beyond his arm's reach drew both of them to look back at him. Not seeming to notice he had become the focus of their attention, he muttered, "Not to be trusted to know where their shoe is, when it's right on their foot. Women."

Sir Philip nodded with relief. "That's likely where it is, then. I was afraid it had gone astray, that someone had it who shouldn't. But your uncle saw to its safety." He looked at her and said, "I will tell no one that I know where it is. Because, in plain fact, I do not."

"And, if anyone asks me, I can truly say that so far as I know, I do not have the book in my possession. What I suspect can remain my own business."

They smiled widely at each other, pleased with that sophistry. A heavy wind shook the windows and a cold draught whispered across the rush matting to startle the fire into burning higher. Frevisse pushed her shoulders back and sat up straighter on the stool. "I've sat here too long. I still have questions to ask. The servers at the feast may be able to tell me something."

Sir Philip sobered, the ease leaving his face. "It isn't something that can just be left. And yet, in some ways, I wish we could leave whoever did it to God's judgment and mercy." That had never entered Frevisse's consideration, and before she could form a reply, he asked, "What made our lord bishop think there was a human rather than the divine hand in Sir Clement's death?"

"He said he had heard Sir Clement demand God's judgment too many other times. He didn't see why this time in particular God should choose to answer him. He wanted to be sure it was God who had chosen this occasion and not someone mortal."

"And now you agree it was someone else, not God. Why?"

Frevisse thought before answering, because she was not sure exactly when or how she had changed her opinion, but finally said, "Partly because it seems an unreasonable way for God to kill a man. A great deal of the lesson for the rest of us was lost by not having him simply die outright at the feast."

"And you presume to understand God's intent in these things?"

Frevisse forebore to acknowledge the jibe. Instead she said, "In the *Cloud of Unknowing* it's said that each person comes to God at a different pace. Today some men who knew Sir Clement said he was changing of late, that he was not so violent as he had been, nor demanded God's judgment so often. Maybe, in his own wickedly slow way, he was coming to God. Would God take a man still deep in sin who was at least beginning to come toward grace?"

"God might," Sir Philip said. "In fact I know he does." He waited and when she did not answer, added, "Those aren't the reasons you're going on with this."

Frevisse watched the fire play among the logs for a while, feeling her way among her own thoughts before saying, "No, they aren't. I want to know what happened. What really happened, not what we imagine happened. I want to know whether there *was* a human hand in this, or if it was indeed God's act against a sinning man."

This time she waited and Sir Philip did not answer. He did not even move but, like her, sat staring into the flames.

Frevisse rubbed her hands over her face where the skin felt dried and tight from the fire's warmth and finally said, "I also remembered the old story of the devil and a summoner traveling together, where the devil refuses to take a cart and horses, though their driver in a bad temper is wishing them to hell. But later when the summoner is tormenting an old woman and she wishes *him* to hell, the devil takes him on the instant because, says the devil, he knows a true wish when he hears it. I wish we could believe that in the moment Sir Clement demanded God's judgment yesterday, he truly wanted it, if only for that single moment, and so God gave it to him. I wish I could believe that. But I don't."

She waited but Sir Philip did not answer. The fire made small sounds in the stillness, and she did not look at him because she knew he was looking at her and she did not want to see his expression.

It was a relief when Dame Perpetua appeared from the shadows of the doorway and said eagerly, breaking the silence between them, "There you are, Dame Frevisse! I've been looking everywhere for you."

"And I came here looking for you," Frevisse returned. She and Sir Philip were both drawn to their feet by Dame Perpetua's obvious excitement. "You found it?"

Smiling with triumph, Dame Perpetua held out a slender volume. "Here, in here, there's exactly what you wanted."

Frevisse took the book from her excitedly. "Why, it's Galen." The master of all doctors, the Roman authority second only to Aesculapius himself.

"Here." Dame Perpetua took the book back and opened it to a place marked by a broken end of quill. "On the right side."

She pointed and Frevisse read. Sir Philip came around to read over her shoulder. When they had finished, he stepped back and they all three looked at one another for a silent moment, until Dame Perpetua said, "It was Master Lionel who found it actually. Found the Galen and said he remembered something was in there about rashes and all."

"I've never heard of such a thing as this," Sir Philip said, indicating the book.

"Nor I, but there it is. Some of what I needed," Frevisse said.

Dame Perpetua's face fell. "Not everything?"

"It tells me in a general way what killed him, but not precisely. Nor who gave it to him. Or how. Though I'm beginning to guess," she added.

Sir Philip looked at her sharply. "You have an idea of the murderer?"

"Oh, dear. I hoped I'd done so well," Dame Perpetua sighed.

Frevisse patted her arm. "You've done wonderfully." She raised her voice. "And so have you, Master Lionel. Thank you."

Dame Perpetua said, "Oh, I forgot to tell you. Word has come that the crowner will be here certainly by late tomorrow morning."

"Then the matter is out of your hands," Sir Philip said to Frevisse.

He was right. The crowner would take what she had learned so far and thank her and dismiss her because there was no place for her, a nun and a woman, in his investigation. Bishop Beaufort would be satisfied. She could return to her grief and to tending her aunt, and be done with Sir Clement's death. But last spring she had used her cleverness to shield the guilty from the law. She would probably never know whether she had been right to do so, or sinfully in error. But here, now, she had chance to make reparation for that by finding out another murderer, more deeply guilty than the one she had protected.

"No," she said in answer to Sir Philip. "I'm not done with this matter yet."

Chapter

🖎 15 🖎

BEAUFORT WAITED AT the window, watching the bleak day. Below him the lead-dull waters of the moat roughened under the wind; beyond the moat, the black, weaving limbs of the elms troubled against the sky. He shivered slightly—the weather was turning more bitter by the hour—and turned back toward the room as one of his clerks ushered in Master Broun, Dame Frevisse, and her companion nun.

Beaufort frowned and sat down in his curved-arm chair without offering his ring to them or the suggestion that they be seated, too. He had expected Dame Frevisse, with inevitably the other nun, but not Master Broun, and did not care for the presumption. Guessing it was hers rather than his, he asked curtly, "You have reason for bringing Master Broun, Dame Frevisse?"

Master Broun showed his surprise. "My lord, I thought you wanted me, that perhaps you felt unwell. The stresses of these past days—"

"I am, thank God, in health." Beaufort made a point of avoiding the attentions of physicians so far as he might. Given a chance, they found things wrong that they claimed needed to be treated in expensive ways that were usually uncomfortable and, in Beaufort's opinion, mostly inefficacious. He understood too well in himself the lure of trying things because one had the power to do so not to recognize the trait in others. "Your being here is Dame Frevisse's doing. She asked to see me."

He fixed her with a look that held contained warning that his time was not to be abused. She bowed her head to him and with admirable brevity said not to him but to Master Broun, "I needed your very expert opinion on a medical matter and thought you would more readily and attentively give it if you understood his grace the cardinal was also interested."

Master Broun again switched his gaze from her to Beaufort. "My lord, I don't understand."

"Nor do I," the cardinal answered, "but I daresay Dame Frevisse is about to enlighten us."

With her head bent a little, her hands neatly folded up her sleeves in front of her, she was an image of respect as she said to Master Broun, "You attended Sir Clement at his death. We spoke of it afterwards, you may remember." Master Broun inclined his head in dignified acknowledgment and stayed silent. She continued, "By things that have been learned since then, it seems that he was poisoned."

Startled, Master Broun hurriedly crossed himself twice while protesting to Beaufort, "Surely, my lord, the hand of God was rarely so clearly seen." He turned to Dame Frevisse. "You saw the red mark of a hand on his face—"

"I didn't," she answered. "I saw only the welts and no pattern at all. Nor did anyone I asked about it. If it was there, only you saw it."

She was plainly as set in her opinion as the physician was in his, and to forestall Master Broun's protest and what might turn to acrimonious debate, Beaufort said, "Is this matter of the hand to the point, Dame?"

"No, my lord."

"Then pass it by." He made that a warning to her and added so Master Broun would equally understand, "I asked Dame Frevisse to look more nearly into the matter of Sir Clement's death and give me her opinion on it. I pray you, heed her and answer what she asks you in your best wise."

His face registering his protest, Master Broun looked sideways at Dame Frevisse and waited.

Her own expression bland and again respectful, she began, "Poison would be the most likely explanation—"

"I assure your grace, there is no such poison," Master Broun interjected. "I am no expert on poisons, I assure you—" His tone indicated that no doctor worth his learning would be expert in such things. "But I am thoroughly familiar with the pharmacopoeia, and there is no drug, no plant, no combination thereof that will cause such symptoms as Sir Clement had." He switched his officiousness to Dame Frevisse. "And I did most clearly see the mark of a hand, as if God smote him on the face." He turned back to Beaufort and assured him, "A most holy and edifying sight before it faded after his death."

"God moves in mysterious ways," Beaufort murmured; and privately added that so did the minds of men. "Dame Frevisse?"

Very mildly—but Beaufort found he was becoming wary of her mildness—Dame Frevisse said, "The *Materia Medica* in Master Chaucer's library agrees completely with what Master Broun has said. I could find no poison that works as this one did."

Master Broun nodded, satisfied.

"But there is this." She withdrew her hands from her

opposite sleeves where she had modestly kept them this while, with a book in one of them. She held it out to Master Broun and said very humbly, "I'm not sure—my Latin is so poor—but there seems something here. Would you look at it?"

Master Broun looked at Beaufort instead, in clear hope of being relieved of so much nonsense. Beaufort nodded toward the book, and, reluctantly, Master Broun took it. There was a marker. He opened to it, and Dame Frevisse reached out to point to a particular place, saying, "It's there. Can you tell us what it says?"

Master Broun instead turned back to the front of the book to find its title. "A work by Galen," he observed.

"Then an authority not to be trifled with," Beaufort said, allowing a trace of his impatience to show. He did not care to be involved in other people's games.

Master Broun set himself promptly to the passage Dame Frevisse had indicated. Beaufort and she waited in silence while he read it through, and then reread it before finally looking up to say in a solemn voice meant to evidence his deep thought and judgment on the matter, "I remember me this passage now from my days at Oxford, but never in all my years at practice have I encountered the matter, to bring it to my mind again until this moment."

"Meaning?" Beaufort asked. He edged the word with sufficient impatience to goad Master Broun to the point.

But Master Broun was bolstered by his expertise now and answered with deliberate consideration, "Meaning that those symptoms evidenced by Sir Clement previous to his death—the stifled breathing, the welts over his face and neck and arms, the great itching—do indeed occur, under certain circumstances from the poison inherent in certain foods."

Impatiently, and more so because Dame Frevisse already knew the answer and was forcing both him and Master Broun through these steps, Beaufort said, "But everything Sir Clement ate and drank at the feast, he shared with others. Didn't he?" he demanded of Dame Frevisse. "Or have you learned otherwise?"

"Everything he ate or drank, others did, too," she agreed.

Master Broun raised an authoritative hand to forestall any other comments. "There are foods, you see—this is very rare, but I remember a fellow student during my time at Oxford would never eat cheese; he said it made him ill and indeed cited Galen on it. I do remember now"—he tapped the book he still held—"that there are foods that in themselves are wholesome in all respects except that in certain people they cause distress precisely such as Sir Clement suffered." He was warming to the subject and went on with enthusiasm. "Even if only touched, they can cause itching and extreme discomfort. And though initial ingestion of whatever particular food afflicts a person may cause only a mild reaction, the effect can be cumulative so that experiencing the food one time too many will bring on symptoms so severe that death will result, though earlier attacks were not fatal."

"And that was why Sir Clement was not terrified when I saw him partly recovered in Sir Philip's room," Frevisse put in. "He had experienced this before and thought he knew what to expect."

"So, in brief," Beaufort said, "there was something at the feast poisonous to Sir Clement but to no one else. He ate of it unknowingly and died."

"I believe that would cover all the facts, yes," Master Broun agreed.

Dame Frevisse said tartly, "So you no longer think it was God who struck him down?"

Master Broun flushed and drew himself up to glare at her as he snapped, "That no longer seems the obvious answer, no."

"Thank you both," Beaufort said crisply, cutting off whatever response Dame Frevisse was opening her mouth to make. "You have been most helpful, Master Broun. Invaluable. You'll receive witness of our pleasure. But pray you both, hold silent on this matter for this while at least."

He made it a request, knowing it would be taken as a command. Master Broun, mollified by the praise and promise of reward, bowed his acceptance. "As your worship wishes."

"Then you have our leave to go. Dame Frevisse, we would have you stay," he added more sternly.

Master Broun cast her a sideways look, satisfied she was in trouble of some sort, and bowed himself from the room. When the door had shut behind the doctor, Beaufort gestured her to sit opposite him, and resting his elbows on the arms of his chair, his hands clasped judiciously in front of him, he regarded her for a while in silence. She sat unruffled under his gaze, more self-contained than some great lords of the realm on whom he had used the same look. He said, "That was well done."

In acknowledgment of his praise, she bent her head and responded, "I doubt he would have been so cooperative except that you were here."

"Which is why you requested my presence. My congratulations. You seem to have mastered many of the frailties of your sex, overcoming even the pride that might have refused to make use of my authority over him. You've dealt with the matter both logically and with some degree of boldness."

He was interested in seeing her reaction, but for a

prolonged moment she held silent, and he found that, like Thomas, her expression was not always easy to read. Then she said evenly, "I've never noticed that pride is particular to either sex, and, by your worship's leave, I've known as many illogical men as I have women, if not more. Nor have I ever thought—despite what the stories say and men seem to admire—that boldness was a virtue if not wisely used."

She said it so politely, with no change of expression or tone, that it was a moment before Beaufort realized she had completely refused his compliment to her on the terms he had given it. Drily, he asked, "You don't care for Aquinas's opinion on the essential frailty of woman's nature?"

"The blessed St. Thomas Aquinas refers to the frailty of her soul's vigor and body's strength, which do not match man's. But we were referring to my mind, and of that St. Thomas says, if I remember correctly, 'The image of God in its principal manifestation—namely, the intellect—is found both in man and woman.'"

"And you see yourself man's equal therefore."

"In worth before the eyes of God, yes. And in our abilities to serve Him, without doubt. But we were made, at the time of creation itself, to be man's handmaid. That at least I will agree to." Unexpectedly she smiled, looking much younger, though her age was impossible to guess in the anonymity of her black habit, close-fitting wimple, and heavy drape of veil. "But in return I think you might be willing to grant the old adage that woman was the last thing God made, and therefore the best."

Beaufort laughed aloud. "That's Thomas's trick, to cut short an argument with a jest completely to the point."

Like Beaufort's, Dame Frevisse's voice was warm with the shared memory of a man they both loved. "He taught me well."

"And yet, with your learning and wit beyond the ordinary, you were willing to give over to Master Broun your solution to Sir Clement's death."

"There are realities that have to be accepted. I've learned to live within such and yet do as well as God has made me able."

"With your God-given intellect that is the equal of a man's."

She acknowledged his teasing by saying with mock solemnity, "Or the better. But no matter how clever we may think I am, the crowner will take the learned evidence of how Sir Clement died far better from Master Broun than he would from me."

Beaufort nodded agreement. "So Sir Clement's death was an accident after all."

"No. I think it was surely murder."

"What?" They had kept their voices pitched low; his immoderate exclamation made several of his clerks look up from their work, and he immediately dropped his voice to order, with no attempt to conceal that he was disconcerted, "Explain that."

"Sir Clement may have known of his affliction. I've heard from several people that there were foods—or a food, I need to ask more specific questions to know exactly—that he wouldn't eat. He sent one of his people to the kitchen here to be sure of what was being served at the feast. He may have known there was something that made him ill and would not have knowingly eaten it. Whatever it was, it had to have been secretly and deliberately put in his food during the feast."

"So Sir Philip may be guilty after all."

"I'm assured that someone is guilty. I doubt it is Sir Philip."

Beaufort raised his eyebrows. "Why?"

"Because he didn't have the opportunity. With this poisoning something would have had to be placed in Sir Clement's food after it left the kitchen. I don't remember that Sir Philip had the chance. And he's told me he has documents that negate any claim Sir Clement might have made against him, so he had no reason, either."

"You believed him when he told you of these documents?"

"It's possible he's lied about them, but it would be a lie too easily discovered for what it was."

"And Sir Philip is not a stupid man. But he could be a desperate one if the documents do not indeed exist, in which case he might have conspired with someone else better able to poison Sir Clement at the feast."

"The three most likely and most able to have done it are Sir Clement's ward, his cousin, and his nephew. They all had opportunity and ample reasons of their own, conspiracy with Sir Philip or not. And there is Sir Philip's brother, who was usher at the feast, if we care to consider Sir Philip did lie about the documents."

"And how do you plan to determine which one of them it may have been, whether alone or with Sir Philip? Or would you rather leave it now to the crowner? He'll be here tomorrow, will take what you've learned and make good use of it, I'm sure."

She hesitated, then answered, "I have some of the pieces needed for an answer, and I think I know how to learn the rest. By your leave, I'd like to go on."

He inclined his head to her gravely. "By my leave you may. And if you need my help in anything with this, ask for it freely."

Chapter
❧ 16 ❧

THE AFTERNOON WAS wearing away, and Frevisse meant to talk to Guy and Lady Anne again, and to Jevan, too. Of everyone around Sir Clement he had gained the most— freedom from his uncle after a lifetime of his cruelties— and lost the most—his livelihood and his hope of Lady Anne; Guy would be taking both from him. Frevisse wanted to know how he was and what he was thinking, not simply because he was part of the question of Sir Clement's death, but because he was a friend of Robert's, and she was fond of Robert, no matter how rarely they saw each other.

But duty and affection took her back to her aunt's bedchamber first. The room was shadowed, the shutters closed, the bed curtains drawn. The women silently at various tasks around the room made shushing gestures at her as she entered. Alice, seated on the window seat with one shutter set a little back so light fell on the book on her lap, beckoned Frevisse to come sit beside her. The gentle puff and pause of Aunt Matilda's breathing came from inside the bed curtains, in token that she was deeply asleep.

"She woke a while ago," Alice whispered, "and ate some broth and milk-soaked bread."

"And you were able to persuade her to sleep again?"

Alice smiled. "Not so much persuaded as gave her no choice. There was a sleeping draught in the wine she drank afterwards. Master Broun says the more she sleeps just now, the better she'll be."

On that at least Frevisse agreed with him. "What of you? If you want to go out for a while, I can watch by her."

Alice shook her head. "This is where I want to be, with Mother and my praying. I'm well enough."

Aware that she had scanted her own prayers all day today, Frevisse glanced down and saw the book her cousin held was indeed a prayer book, opened to the psalms in Latin. That reminded her of the Wycliffe book in its bundle somewhere among her things across the room. Taking her mind quickly away from the mingled guilt and pleasure of that thought, she asked, "Is there anything you need done that I can do for you?"

"Mother was worrying over Sir Clement's family, anxious that someone express our formal sympathy for their loss. Would you go to them, to give them our sympathy, and explain why neither Mother nor I came instead? I'd ask William to go but he won't. He simply wants anything to do with Sir Clement out from under his way."

"I'll do it gladly." Frevisse forbore to add that she had been going to them anyway. "Though I fear that neither they nor anyone else are overwhelmed by grief. Sir Clement wasn't loved."

"God keep us from a like end," said Alice. "It was a fearful thing to see, and to know he'd called it down upon himself."

They both crossed themselves. But Frevisse added, to lighten Alice's mood, "Still, he'd worked long and hard for it, setting everyone else against him along the way."

"That's true," Alice agreed with a trace of amusement. "He even managed between Father's death and his own to set my lord husband against him with no great difficulty."

"How?" Frevisse asked, surprised.

"By bringing up that property dispute he had with Father. He wouldn't let it rest even this little while of the funeral. William was furious over the rudeness, and because even though there's no matter in it, the lawyers' fees would mount nonetheless, if it went that far."

"I doubt there's anyone who's sorry he's dead."

"Certainly not William. Well, the crowner will be here tomorrow, I hear, and that will be the end of it. I trust Sir Clement's family will leave with his body immediately once they're allowed to?"

"I understand so."

"I've told Master Gallard to tell them we'll give any help we can."

"And please ask me for anything I can do, at any time."

"Your prayers," Alice said, smiling. "Surely your prayers are what I want most. And your friendship," she added to her own evident surprise as much as Frevisse's.

Frevisse smiled back at her, aware of growing affection for this cousin she hardly knew. "You'll have both, without fail. I think I should like to have your friendship, now that I'm not forever being annoyed by you," she added teasingly.

"Annoyed by me? How?" Alice demanded, amused as Frevisse had meant for her to be.

"Because you could sit for hours at your sewing or whatever other task your mother gave you and never make the least bother about it. You always seemed very content with yourself, while I was ever wishing I was being or doing something else."

"Except when you were reading," Alice said shrewdly.

"Except when I was reading," Frevisse agreed, and they both laughed. They were quickly shushed by Aunt Matilda's women and ducked their heads to hide more laughter behind their hands.

Then Alice confessed in a whisper, "I was always annoyed by you, too. You'd been everywhere and seen everything, it seemed, and Father never seemed to mind how much time you spent among his books. It wasn't until after you were gone that I dared begin to press him as you did for books."

"I never knew you were interested."

"I wasn't supposed to be. I was my mother's daughter and there was the end of it."

"But you didn't let it be the end of it."

"No," Alice said firmly. "I did not."

Frevisse's smile widened. "Oh, yes, I think we can be very good friends indeed."

Frevisse found Lady Anne alone in her room, except for her two maids, and like Alice, she was seated at the window, a book open on her lap, while her maids sorted through belongings in her traveling chest. The cold gray daylight gave her usual blond loveliness an ashen appearance, but even allowing for that, she looked pale, delicately shadowed under her eyes as if she had not slept so well as could be wished.

Frevisse, as she approached her, was surprised to see the book was another prayer book, and opened to the Office of the Dead. Lady Anne, catching her glance and the surprise in it, said, "I found myself wondering if there might be hope of Sir Clement's salvation after all. I thought how unpleasant it would be to eventually arrive in purgatory and find him waiting for us."

"I suspect that if Sir Clement manages to go so far as purgatory, he'll be far too busy with his own redemption to trouble yours."

Frevisse's irony was lost on Lady Anne. She merely considered the thought for a moment, then answered, "I suppose you're right." She closed the book and tossed it toward one of her maidservants. "Sit down, if you please."

Frevisse suspected that Lady Anne's manners depended on her mood and possibly on the importance of whom she was talking to, because no matter how young and vulnerable she looked, seated there pale in the winter light with the tender shadows under her eyes, she clearly had a strong core of self-will and self-interest that had small consideration for others beyond how they affected her directly.

Frevisse sat, folded her hands into her sleeves, and said mildly, "I trust there is always hope of heaven for all of us, even someone so outwardly without grace as Sir Clement."

"It wasn't merely outwardly. He delighted in the sorrows of others. Besides, God wouldn't have struck him down like that if he weren't deserving of it." Lady Anne said it flatly, with no particular venom. Sir Clement was no longer a problem to her; she would shortly have dismissed him completely from her life. But in consideration of Frevisse, she added, "Though, of course, we should hope the best for him. You've probably been praying for him. You've given your life over to such charity of spirit."

"To the will of God, rather," Frevisse said.

Lady Anne drew her delicate brows together in a pretty frown. "It must be very strange to give yourself up so completely. To the will of your prioress, the will of your abbott, the will of your bishop. I suppose you even have to listen to the pope. You have no life of your own at all!"

"One grows use to it," Frevisse said, amused by the girl's

complete incomprehension. "Even to the pope. That is the core trouble with giving yourself up to the will of God—it requires you also give yourself up to the will of people who are not always godlike."

"I suppose it makes you far more sure of heaven," Lady Anne said doubtfully. She obviously thought she would find a better way to that goal than through so much sacrifice. She was also growing a little bored with the conversation, fretting her white fingers at her skirts.

"Actually I've come from Countess Alice and her mother and husband, to express our deep sympathy for your loss and assure you of any help that they can give during your stay here."

Lady Anne brightened. "How very kind. He's important at court, isn't he? The earl of Suffolk? And much more charming than that dreadful Bishop of Winchester."

"I believe so, yes," Frevisse said in general answer.

"But have you heard when the crowner is supposed to arrive? This waiting is terribly tedious."

"Tomorrow for certain."

"And then we can go home and be married and be rid of everything that might ever remind us of Sir Clement! Won't that be grand!"

"My lady?" Guy asked from the doorway.

The maidservants rose from their work to curtsy to him. Lady Anne sprang to her feet and went to him, saying gladly, "Dame Frevisse came to offer us the family's condolences on Sir Clement's death, and she says the crowner will be here certainly tomorrow. Then we'll be able to go home!"

"When he's finished his questioning," Frevisse reminded her.

Lady Anne waved a dismissive hand. "There's hardly

anything to question. There's Sir Clement dead and God did it. We all saw it."

Frevisse had risen at Guy's coming. Now, smiling in her best and most modest nun wise, she sat down. Lady Anne cast her a look as if willing her to understand she could leave now and everyone would be pleased, but Frevisse feigned not to see it, and with no choice, they joined her, Lady Anne's displeasure somewhat showing. Frevisse smiled on them both and said, "My cousin the countess of Suffolk asked me to tell you that if there is aught we can do for you, you have but to ask."

As she expected, the mention of her cousin brought Guy's attention to her more respectfully. "Thank her grace for her kindness. We're doing very well. Everything considered," he added, remembering there should be some grief, if only for appearance's sake. "Everything has been seen to and is ready. As soon as the crowner gives permission, we'll be able to leave."

Judging by the warm glance that passed between him and Lady Anne, he would have taken her hands then in the shared pleasure of that coming freedom, if Frevisse had not been there.

She would have gladly left them to it but she still had questions she needed answered. "Was Sir Clement's property all entailed, so it comes directly to you, or will there be provisions in his will lessening the inheritance?"

"It's all entailed," Guy said cheerfully. "He was too busy with his quarrels to spend time extending his holdings. It all comes to me."

"With surely some provision made for Jevan Dey as his only other relation. Jevan *is* his only other relative, isn't he?"

"He is, but there's no provision for him. Sir Clement was clear about that all along."

"But he served him so well, from what I've heard and seen. Why, even at the funeral feast, no one but Jevan waited on him. Or did they?"

"Only old Jevan."

"Except for the wine. That was somebody else," Lady Anne said.

"He was pouring for everyone along that part of the table," Guy said. "But the food, only Jevan brought that. Serviceable to the last, for all the good it will do him. No, everything comes to me, and Jevan will have exactly what he's earned all these years of licking Sir Clement's boots."

"And payment in full for putting you in trouble with Sir Clement when he could," Lady Anne added. "That beastly marchpane."

"That, too," Guy agreed.

"The marchpane?" Frevisse asked. "You mentioned that before, didn't you?"

"Jevan suggested he give it to Sir Clement when Guy asked him what a good gift would be. And Sir Clement was rude about it ever afterwards."

"But Jevan might have done it innocently, not knowing it would enrage Sir Clement," Frevisse suggested.

"I doubt my cousin ever does anything innocently. He meant to make trouble then as surely as Sir Clement ever did. As they say, 'Like in one way, like in more,' and they were alike in more than looks." Guy frowned. "No, when Jevan has shown me what I need to know of the manor's matters, I'll be rid of him. There's no other way."

Frevisse put on a thoughtful expression. "Lady Anne and I were talking of Sir Clement's salvation before you came in." Guy smothered a rude noise. Frevisse pretended not to hear, but went on as if she had been considering the problem of Sir Clement's soul. "Is there any chance he was not so far in sin as we all think he was? Had he shown any inclination of late toward repenting his ways?"

Lady Anne answered, "I think he may have been a little less quarrelsome of late, but I also think that was simply because he was growing old and lacked the strength toward it he had had."

"But he hadn't been ill? He wasn't given to illness?"

"Sir Clement?" Guy scoffed. "Never. Not even rheums in winter. Nothing made him ill."

Frevisse looked to Lady Anne. "You found that true?"

"Oh, yes. He was always concerned over himself. Wouldn't eat this unless it was perfectly fresh, wouldn't eat that at all, had to have things cooked just so. But ill, no, never."

"What sort of foods didn't he like?" Frevisse pressed.

Lady Anne shrugged. "Anything that happened to go against his fancy. From one time to the next he could hate a thing or love it. There wasn't any sense to it."

Guy nodded agreement. "He was impossible to please."

Frevisse made casual conversation awhile longer for the sake of seeming polite, but could find no way to elicit any more useful information from either of them. She made a graceful departure as soon as she was sure of that, with some hope of finding Jevan, until she realized supper time was more near than she had thought. For manners' sake, she ought to dine in the parlor with whomever of the family came, and so she went that way instead of after Jevan.

Aunt Matilda did not rise for the meal. "But she's awake and, I think, better," Alice said. "Sir Philip is with her for a while now so I could leave."

She was serene but wan, and the earl, elegant in his

mourning black, was attentive to her at the table, seeing she had the finest and daintiest of every dish and gently insisting she eat and drink more than she might have otherwise. For the first time, in his kindness to her cousin, Frevisse found something particular about him that she liked. But it meant that, since Bishop Beaufort had chosen to dine in his own rooms, and Sir Philip was with Aunt Matilda, there were only she and Dame Perpetua to make other conversation; and since the one thing they both wished to speak of was impossible here, their conversation was slight, with many silences. In them, Frevisse followed her own thoughts.

Despite all her questioning, she still had only pieces, like the shards of a window she had once seen outside a burned church. Slivers and cracked pieces of bright colors, with here and there a recognizable part of a face, or the fold of a robe, or the petals of a flower, but most of it making no sense at all, just pieces that might never have been part of any pattern.

But there had to be a way here to bring all the pieces into sense. She knew Sir Clement had died from eating a food that was poison to him but to no one else around him. She did not know what the food was; or how he had come to eat it, since he seemed to have known exactly what was dangerous to him; or who had given it to him; or exactly why. The why was the least problem; there were more than enough people with reasons for hating Sir Clement to death. But who had known exactly what to use to kill him? And how had they put it into his food at the feast? Guy, Lady Anne, and Jevan were the three best able to have done it, and they all had reasons to want him dead. Neither Guy nor Lady Anne apparently had any idea there was a food deadly to Sir Clement; or they—one or the other or both—were feigning their innocence. If they were not, that left Jevan, except he was going to lose the most by Sir Clement's death and so, perhaps, should have been least willing toward it.

She realized Dame Perpetua had been talking to her, attempting to maintain at least the appearance of propriety, and that she had been nodding her head as if attending to what she said. But now something finally meshed with her own thoughts and she interrupted sharply. "What?"

Dame Perpetua paused in mild surprise at the abruptness, then repeated patiently, "I said that I'm sorry I delayed your learning about the poison this afternoon by not staying where you expected to find me."

"No, that was all right," Frevisse assured her. "It was what you said after that. About why you left."

"Because someone came in to see Sir Philip."

"No, you said who it was that came in."

"Why, Sir Clement's nephew. The one who looks so like him. He seemed troubled, or maybe only tired, but he wanted to speak to Sir Philip alone. I thought it would be easier for me to go than them, so I went in search of you, with the Galen."

"And he stayed to talk with Sir Philip?"

"That's why he came," Dame Perpetua explained again, patiently.

Sir Philip had been talking with Jevan, then, probably not long before she had come into the library herself, but he had never mentioned Jevan being there. *Why should he?* she asked herself. And promptly asked back, *Why hadn't he?* Especially after she had told him what she was doing at Bishop Beaufort's behest, when he had to know that she would be interested in anything about anyone who had been around Sir Clement.

The meal was finished. Alice and Suffolk were rising; the servants were hovering to clear dishes and table away.

Frevisse stood up with Dame Perpetua and said, "If you'll pardon us, we're going to do Vespers in the chapel, to make up for the services we have somewhat scanted these few days."

No objection could be made to that, except perhaps by Dame Perpetua, who had had no idea of any such thing. But she remained admirably silent, made her curtsy with Frevisse, and followed her from the room. Not until they were on the stairs down to the hall did she say, "This is a good idea of yours, Dame. But what else are you about?"

"I don't know," Frevisse said. "But I couldn't stay there longer, doing nothing."

"It seems you've already done a great deal today."

"But none of it will matter if I don't find out the answers that make all of it make sense."

"You might be better for a rest, a night's sleep."

"I might be," Frevisse agreed, and went on. With a sigh, Dame Perpetua accompanied her.

The servants were just finishing with clearing the hall after supper. Frevisse saw Lady Anne and Guy, Sir Ralph, Sir Edward, and Lady Eleanor clustered in front of the fireplace, but her attention went to Master Gallard, busy at setting servants to make the rushes even where they had been scrabbled by table legs and people's feet. For all his apparent fluster, he was efficient about it, just as he had been efficient at everything these past few days. But even now that she knew he was Sir Philip's brother, she could find no family resemblance, either in looks or manner.

He saw her before she could turn away, and hurried over, to make his eager, bobbing bow and ask, "Is there aught I can do for you? How does Mistress Chaucer? Better, I hope. This has been a very heavy business for her, poor lady."

"She's resting quietly and that's the best thing for her just now."

"Very certainly. But is there anything I can do for you?"

She had been intending to ask Guy and Lady Anne where Jevan might be, since he was not in the hall, but now she said, "I'm looking for Jevan Dey."

Master Gallard puckered his lips thoughtfully, then said, "I think I saw him going to the chapel before supper. He never came to eat, you know. He should. He's far too thin. Unless he's gone somewhere else, he's in the chapel, surely."

"There's very little that you miss, is there, Master Gallard?"

Frevisse said it as a compliment, and he took it so. "No, no, not if I can help it."

"I didn't know you were Sir Philip's brother."

Master Gallard looked surprised. "There was no call for you to know, certainly. And there's very little like between us, is there?"

"But you're glad to be serving together this while?"

"Most certainly. We were apart for many years, but have a fondness for each other. It's good to be together while we can, before—" He broke off with a sudden intake of breath, as if he had nearly committed an indiscretion.

"Until Bishop Beaufort takes him into his service," Frevisse finished for him.

Master Gallard looked relieved. "You know his expectations then? Yes, he has good hope of it. And well he should. He's very clever."

"And ambitious?" She said it as a mild joke about something of which they both knew and approved.

Master Gallard bobbed on his feet as he answered archly, "Within the limits he deserves to be, surely."

"Wasn't he bothered by Sir Clement's insistence he could prove you weren't freeborn?"

"It was all nonsense. Pigeon traps in water." Master Gallard waved his hands airily to show the foolishness. "There are papers. Philip has them all. Sir Clement had no claim, even on me. Philip would be safe, of course, being a priest, but I'd have no protection at all, and can you see me in a village, doing day work for anyone? But there were no grounds for it. Sir Clement was only being odious."

"But you're nonetheless not sorry that he's dead."

"There's no one sorry, I fear." Master Gallard dropped his voice to emphasize the solemnity of his answer. "And few pretending they are. Though after a death like that we should all consider our place in God's eye and amend our ways."

"You were in the hall when it happened?" Frevisse could not remember whether she had seen him then or not.

"No, no. My feet, you know"—Master Gallard bobbed slightly—"they grow sore when I'm on them too long, or if I stand too still. They're very tender, and that morning by the time we'd finished with the funeral and seeing everyone into their places, well, I was in desperate need of sitting down, and I did, in the kitchen where I could still be sure of what went on, of course, in case of need. But when the outcry over Sir Clement began, it took me too long to reach the hall, with the servants in the way and all, so I only saw him being taken out. But there was talk of it afterward. More than enough talk. A terrible business, terrible. You've recovered from the shock of seeing it, my ladies?"

"Quite recovered, yes," Frevisse assured him. "If you'll excuse us?"

Master Gallard assured them that he would, and while he

was busy at it, Frevisse deftly extricated herself and Dame Perpetua and they went on their way.

"Did you learn anything from that?" Dame Perpetua asked when they were well away from being overheard.

"I learned Master Gallard agrees with Sir Philip's story that Sir Clement was no threat to them. It would be better if he'd said he'd actually seen the papers that insure that. So far, I have only Sir Philip's word that they exist."

"And you couldn't very well ask Master Gallard."

"No. That's something I'll have to leave to the crowner. He has a right to ask and be answered, where I might be refused for impertinence. But I also learned Master Gallard was in the kitchen and so had access to Sir Clement's food." Which was useless unless she found some way he could have known which dishes Jevan would take to Sir Clement, because surely he could not have put the poison food into every dish or even remove one without someone in the kitchen noticing what he was doing, and that would have been too large a risk to run.

The chapel was as it had been the first evening, when Frevisse had come to pray beside Chaucer's corpse, except that there were fewer candles around the bier and only two men kneeled beside the coffin. One of them was Jevan.

Not willing to disturb him at his prayers, Frevisse beckoned Dame Perpetua to the other end of the chapel, and by a single candle's light, their heads close together over Dame Perpetua's prayer book, they whispered through Vespers. When they were done, Dame Perpetua looked questioningly from Frevisse to Jevan's back, and back again. Frevisse shrugged, not knowing what to do except wait and hope it would not be too long.

It was not. The chapel's chill had barely begun to be uncomfortable before Jevan straightened stiffly and rose slowly to his feet. As he bowed to the altar, Frevisse went forward so that when he turned away, she was standing beside him.

"Master Jevan."

"Dame Frevisse." He bowed again. He was tired; it showed in his face and the way he held himself.

"I need to talk to you." She indicated the door, and he followed her out into the antechamber.

But when she stopped, he said, "I have duties I must needs go to."

"I'll keep you only briefly. My cousin Countess Alice has asked I give her sympathies to Sir Clement's family, since she's nursing her mother presently, and to assure you of any help you need in your while here."

"The lady is very gracious. I hope Mistress Chaucer isn't badly ill?"

"Not ill so much as worn out with trying to be brave through everything."

"But she's better?"

"We think so."

"That's well then." Jevan clearly considered the conversation finished. He began to bow again, to leave. To forestall this, Frevisse said, "I've heard a great deal about your uncle and what he was like. It's to your credit you were praying for him."

A dull flush spread over Jevan's face. Was he that unused to compliments? Frevisse wondered. But he only said, "He should be prayed for by someone, and who better than I?"

"Still, he wasn't an easy man to be around. No one seems sorry at all that he's dead. Are you?"

"Not in the slightest." The answer came with the firmness of deep conviction. "Everyone around him will be better for being rid of him."

"Especially Guy and Lady Anne."

Jevan's jaw tightened, but he did not flinch. "They'll have their desires now, and God give them joy of it."

"And you? What will you do? Go on in service to Guy? I gather you were invaluable to Sir Clement."

"I was his drudge," Jevan said.

"You could have left him, found work elsewhere."

Jevan shook his head. "He left me no hope of that. I tried once, took work as a wool packer for one of the merchants who bought our wool. Sir Clement hunted me down and gave neither me nor the merchant peace until finally the man had to let me go, to be rid of him. Sir Clement said he would do that whenever I tried to leave."

"At least Guy will be an easier master."

"At his first chance, Guy will have me out the door and down the road with a curse and not much else to carry with me. We don't like each other."

"He still holds the marchpane trick against you."

Brief pleasure flickered on Jevan's face. "There were walnut halves set in the center of each piece. Sir Clement all but foamed at the mouth when he saw them and never forgave him. He'd boil into a temper every time he saw Guy after that."

As if with only mild, gossiping curiosity, Frevisse asked, "But why?"

Jevan's face had fallen back into its settled expression of endurance. "Walnuts made Sir Clement ill. Guy didn't know that."

"But after the marchpane, everyone in shouting distance of Sir Clement probably did," Frevisse said, remembering his temper.

"Easily," Jevan agreed grimly.

As if in simple commiseration, containing her satisfaction

at having at last another part of what she needed to know, and wanting more, Frevisse said, "Sir Clement had a finicking stomach, I've heard. The milk had to be fresh. The goblet couldn't be pewter. He didn't like nuts. The cook was telling me. Was Sir Clement feigning or did any of that really make him ill?"

"Some things, yes, though not as many as he pretended. Walnuts did. Even touching them—" Jevan broke off with a shake of his head. "My lady, I dislike talking about him, and I have things that need to be done. If you'll excuse me."

"My pardon. Certainly. I forget myself and chatter overmuch," Frevisse said. "Thank you for your kindness. And remember my cousin's offer. Anything you may need while at Ewelme . . ."

Jevan had retreated while she was still talking. She trailed off to silence and stood gazing at the air in front of her, considering.

Chapter

🔸 17 🔹

Overnight, HOARFROST HAD whitened the world—grass and trees and roofs prickled with it. Ice rimmed the black moat waters. A haze blurred the nearer trees; there were no distances. The cold that had crept around the window edges yesterday now thrust deeply into the parlor, so that the comfort of the fire was barely felt beyond an arm's length from the flames.

Warm in his ample robes of fine wool, the outermost one magnificently fur-lined, Beaufort had chosen to sit at the room's far end, where he could watch everyone as they entered, and when they had greeted him and respectfully kissed his episcopal ring and moved away, observe them while they moved and talked among themselves.

Dame Frevisse had come to him last night, had asked him to arrange this gathering under the guise that Countess Alice wished to ease the enforced stay of both Sir Clement's family and the three other guests waiting to testify to the crowner. Beaufort had suggested to Dame Frevisse then that she might prefer to leave the matter now to the crowner's hand. "Master Geoffrey is competent. He'll make the best use of whatever you have, and thank you for it. You've done sufficiently, and I thank you," he had told her.

She had bent her head respectfully but answered, "By your leave, this is a thing I'd like to finish if I may."

"And you think you can by bringing them all together?"

"All together and unsuspecting. Yes, I think so."

There had been various arguments he could have raised, or he could have simply refused, but her firmness of purpose and cleverness in the matter so far had both amused and interested him. He wanted to know how much more she could do, and had seen to Countess Alice's agreement without explaining to her why he had asked the favor.

So they were all here now, with Dame Frevisse sitting quietly to one side with the other nun, both of them drawn into the anonymity of their habits and veils. Beaufort carefully cast them no more than a rare glance, but he judged that Dame Frevisse was watching the others around the room as carefully as he was. And with more knowledge of them than he had, for she had not fully explained either what she had learned with her questioning or what she intended to do this morning. He had begun to find her intelligence and her strong, carefully controlled will disconcerting, as he had always found Thomas's.

The two knights and lady who were there simply because they had sat too near Sir Clement at the feast, were talking with Suffolk. Beaufort gave them scant attention; he had gathered that neither they nor Suffolk had any part in Dame Frevisse's suspicions.

Countess Alice, her mourning black becoming to her fairness, was standing with Lady Anne, their two heads leaned close together, the girl listening and nodding wide-eyed to what Countess Alice was saying. She was a pretty child, but Beaufort was not much moved by prettiness. It was a fleeting thing; hers would probably not outlast her youth, a fact that had undoubtedly escaped the young fool who intended to marry her. He was standing beside her now, clearly proud that she was his.

The nephew who would have nothing out of Sir Clement's death stood apart from everyone else, Beaufort noted. He held a goblet of the warmed, spiced wine the servants were passing around and was watching one person and then another in the talk around him. It was a pity that he looked so like his uncle; that alone would be enough to set people against him. Though he looked like his mother, too, come to that. Beaufort had known her slightly, and how a long-jawed woman with a temper that matched her brother's had ever managed to marry for love was beyond Beaufort's understanding, but she had. And in the long run fairly well ruined her son's life by doing so. The only thing young Dey had brought out of the wreck others had made of his life so far was his apparent dispassion.

Which was more than that usher fellow had, standing there by the door, bustling servants in and out. Beaufort wished it were possible to put something heavy on his head to hold him flat on his feet for a while. Why had Matilda chosen such a creature?

At least she was not here. She showed no sign yet of rising from her bed, and no one had suggested that she should.

Sir Philip came in behind another servant bringing a tray of small tarts—if nothing else, they'd be well-fed when this was done. Yesterday Dame Frevisse had seemed sure Sir Philip was clear of the murder. She had seemed less sure last evening, to Beaufort's concealed annoyance. Sir Philip was too clever and too potentially useful a man to lose if it could be helped.

Beaufort watched as the priest paused to speak to young Dey, too low to be heard, and then came on to make his obeisance. Beaufort received it absently, noting over his shoulder that whatever he had said to young Dey, it brought no change to Dey's face. The young man had not even nodded or answered, only taken a tart from the servant waiting beside him with the absent gesture of someone hoping to be left alone.

With Sir Philip's arrival, everyone expected was here. Beaufort looked toward Dame Frevisse. She raised her head to meet his gaze and with the slightest downward twitch of it told him she was ready for him to begin. Hoping she indeed knew what she was about, Beaufort rose.

Everyone's attention came around to him, their conversations falling away to silence. He waited until the quiet was complete and even a little drawn-out, then said, "You have not wondered why you were all asked here, thinking it was only for courtesy's sake. But there was other purpose in it. I pray you, give heed to Dame Frevisse."

He sat down again, and every head turned toward her. Rising in turn, hands folded into her sleeves, her expression mild, she said in a clear, carrying voice to all of them together, "His grace the cardinal bishop of Winchester has believed from the very first that Sir Clement did not die by God's hand but was murdered."

Various degrees of consternation and surprise showed on every face, but Dame Frevisse went steadily on and no one spoke out.

"He asked me to learn what I could of how he was killed and by whom. In some ways, I've learned a great deal. In others, not enough. There were very many people who disliked Sir Clement, and some who hated him, who probably hate him even now. But of those, only a few had chance to strike at him during the feast, and all of those who had that chance are here now."

While the others mostly glanced around at each other with rousing alarm, Suffolk took a step toward her and said with authority suitably edged with indignation, "You're saying that you accuse one of us of killing him?"

"Yes."

Suffolk opened his mouth to respond, but Beaufort quietly raised the fingers of his right hand from the curve of the chair arm, and Suffolk subsided. Dame Frevisse continued, "It had to be someone well aware of Sir Clement's penchant for asking God to strike him down. That could be anyone who had ever been around him any length of time. But it also had to have been someone able to poison him at the feast."

The word "poison" whispered around the room from one to another. Dame Frevisse's gaze traveled impartially over everyone there, taking in their varied expressions. Beaufort could not tell if she lingered on one longer than the others. "I considered that he might have been actually ill or even touched by God at the feast, and only poisoned later in the room where he was taken to recover. But from what I've learned, he was surely poisoned at the feast, in front of all of us, by someone able to take advantage of the moment when he would almost certainly demand God's judgment. Someone who knew about a poison so specific to Sir Clement that no one else would be harmed by it, whoever ate with him."

Suffolk exclaimed, "That's nonsense! There's no poison that specific!"

"There is," interposed Beaufort. "We have authority for it. And she has my authority to continue."

They exchanged glances, and Dame Frevisse said, "For a great many people, Sir Clement was only an annoyance, to be tolerated when he couldn't be avoided. For others, he was a very real danger. Sir Philip—" Startled gazes turned on the priest where he stood to one side of the room. He met them with a slight bow of his head and a calm expression. "—was threatened by Sir Clement's assertion that he was born unfree. And so was his brother, Master Gallard, and while Sir Philip seems to have had no way to come at Sir Clement's food during the feast, Master Gallard very definitely did."

Master Gallard gaped at her from the doorway, switched his shocked look to his brother, and returned his stare to Dame Frevisse, his mouth working at unvoiced protests.

"Then there is Jevan Dey, who served Sir Clement all through the feast, handled every dish that went to him, and hated him perhaps more fully than anyone."

Jevan met the looks turned his way with the same dispassion he had shown before.

"Lady Anne, who sat next to Sir Clement at the feast, had every dish within her reach once it was served. And the goblet they both drank from. She loathed Sir Clement—"

"And still do," Lady Anne said fiercely. Guy took hold of her hand, warning her to silence, but she went on, "I hope he's burning deep in hell!"

Beaufort said, "That's as may be, but not the question here."

Dame Frevisse continued relentlessly. "If she went against Sir Clement's will in her choice of marriage while still in his wardship, he could have ruined her with all the fines the law allows in such a matter. Worse, if he forced her to marry him, she could never marry Guy, her own choice. She had compelling reason to want Sir Clement dead as soon as might be."

"Then so did I!" Guy put his arm possessively, protectively, around Lady Anne's waist.

"Yes," Dame Frevisse agreed. "And seated as you both were, on either side of him, you could have worked together, one of you distracting him while the other put the walnuts in—what? The meat pie? Finely ground, they would have gone unnoticed—"

Sir Philip's sharp movement broke across her words. He closed the distance between himself and Jevan in a single stride, seized Jevan's wrist and jerked it down, away from his mouth. In rigid, silent struggle, Jevan pulled against his hold. But Dame Frevisse must have seen him move nearly as soon as Sir Philip had; she was there, taking the unbitten tart out of Jevan's hand.

"No," she said gently. "No more, Jevan. Not sin added to sin."

With a deep, shuddering breath, Jevan went slack in Sir Philip's hold. His eyes were no longer expressionless but bitter and exhausted and hopeless all together as he looked at her and said, "Don't you suppose it might be a mercy? To die as he did could be expiation of a kind."

"To die by your own hand is damnation," Sir Philip returned, still holding on to him.

Jevan threw back his head, like a runner at race's end trying to draw breath enough to steady himself. His chest heaved with his effort, and then he said in a voice cruelly edged with pain, "I was born in the wane of the moon, when everything goes assward!"

He looked across the little distance to Lady Anne, and the

cruelty was gone into great gentleness. "I've bought your happiness for you. May you live gladly in it."

"Oh, Jevan!" Lady Anne cried out. "You killed him!" Her words broke the blank incomprehension on Guy's face. He started for Jevan with clenched fists rising. "You killed him and meant to make it seem I did it! You belly-crawling cur, I—"

Master Gallard came in front of him, stopping him with a hold on his arm that Guy, with his first angry tug against it, discovered he could not break.

"No." Dame Frevisse cut her voice across Guy's. "That's exactly what he never meant to happen." She was still looking only at Jevan, with a sadness Beaufort did not understand. And Jevan was looking back at her, the two of them alone with what she had to say, despite the people all around them. "You took great trouble and waited a long while, I'd guess, for the chance to kill Sir Clement in a way that would keep suspicion away from everyone. A great feast with many people present, where Sir Clement would inevitably find occasion to stand up and demand God's judgment on himself, and no one suspected of his death when it came because how likely was it any of us had seen a man die the way Sir Clement did? Isn't that how you meant it to be? And when you realized here that you'd failed, that we knew it was murder after all, you meant to eat that tart full of walnuts, and die the way he did."

To her and no one else, Jevan said, "When I was small, he ate some once by accident. I saw what they did to him. It made him angry, both that it happened and that I saw him that way. So he made me eat some, forced them down me, and laughed when I broke out in the rash and itching. His was worse, but he said it was like that, that it had happened to him before and each time it was worse. It happened one other time, later. He nearly died of it then, so I hoped that if it happened again, it would kill him."

"And when you decided you couldn't bear him alive anymore, for your own sake and for Lady Anne, you remembered," Dame Frevisse said.

"I remembered. And waited, as you said, a long while, with the packet of ground nuts in my belt pouch, until I saw what I thought was my chance." He spoke almost as if by rote, as if the thing had grown dull with repeating to himself too many times. "I saw the meat pies being made when I talked to the cook that morning. Their crusts were blind-baked, the top crust separate from the bottom, the filling put in later. The top crust was only set on, not sealed. In the crowding and hurry of serving, it was easy to bump the top of Sir Clement's pie awry and step aside as if to set it right. What I did instead . . ." His control wavered, and he paused to draw a steadying breath. "What I did instead, with my back to everyone, was scatter the walnuts—I had them ready in my hand—over the meat filling and put the crust back on. No one was likely to notice me enough to remember I'd even done it, or think it mattered, if they did."

"But in the room, when he began to be better, how did you poison him again?" Dame Frevisse asked.

"I didn't. It's taken him that way before, seeming to ease and then coming on again. And this time it came on strongly enough to kill him."

"You meant for us to believe it was God who killed him!" Suffolk said indignantly.

Murmurs and exclamations of anger or shock began to run among everyone in the room, but Beaufort bore over them with, "Why did you do it? No matter how much you hated him, you had so little to gain from his death. Certainly not enough to so imperil your soul. Why did you do it?"

In a proud, dead voice, Jevan said, "I had no hope anymore for myself, whether he was dead or living. But I could set her free to go where her heart wants to."

"But Jevan . . ." Lady Anne, in the circle of Guy's arm, reached uncertainly for words. "You know I love Guy. That I've always loved him. That I don't love you."

With a brilliance of pain in his eyes seared by cold hopelessness, Jevan answered, "I know," and looked away.

Darkness drew in early under the close sky, and the freezing cold crept with it. There was no fire in Chaucer's library now, and Frevisse and Dame Perpetua sat close together, saying Compline by a single candle's light among the shadows. They had come here because Frevisse needed time away from all the day's demands. Jevan's confession had only been the beginning. At Suffolk's orders, he had been taken under guard to be kept for the crowner's coming, but Frevisse had had to stay and deal with everyone else's questions, until word came that rumor of what had passed had reached Aunt Matilda and she wished her niece's presence.

Then everything had had to be repeated and explained again. But at the end of it, Aunt Matilda had been sitting up in bed, eating broth and bread with more vigor than she had shown in days while exclaiming over the rudeness of committing murder at a funeral. "Though if someone was going to be murdered, Sir Clement was the best choice. I never liked him."

The crowner's arrival had been announced then, and Frevisse had been summoned to his presence and Bishop Beaufort's. He had proved to be a quiet, listening man, and she had detailed everything for him more deeply than she had to anyone else, down to why she had set the trap as she had.

"Among the three best able to poison Sir Clement, there was no way to prove who did it, no way to disprove any denial they might make. Jevan told me himself that walnuts made his uncle ill. That made me think he might be innocent. But then again, he could simply not have been careful to conceal it because he didn't know there was any suspicion of murder and so a need for silence. On the other hand, Guy and Lady Anne's silence about the nuts could have been innocence—they didn't know it was important and so said nothing—or guilt—a concealing of a dangerous fact. There was no way to tell. What I did know was that according to Galen even touching a food that ill affects a person the way these nuts did Sir Clement can bring on a rash and itching. I remembered that at Sir Clement's death, while we stood nervously around, someone was rubbing his hand against his thigh. Rubbing and rubbing as if with nerves. Or with a terrible itching. I could remember that but not who it had been. Guy or Jevan, I thought, but it made me think the murderer might, like Sir Clement, be made ill by the nuts, that he had handled them at least briefly and been affected. So I asked for everyone to be brought together, and had the cook make tarts with walnuts in them, not plainly but so that someone would have to be holding one before he noticed. Then I watched to see who would take one and not eat it."

"And Jevan Dey did not," the crowner said.

"Jevan Dey did not." And so she had found her murderer. And nearly lost him when he realized that his attempt to keep everyone from suspicion had failed and tried to die the death he had given his uncle.

What she did not know yet was how Sir Philip had known to stop him in time.

But meanwhile, she had given a murderer over to justice, and in some part of her, that was the beginning of reparation for her choices of last spring. But in her mind she still saw Jevan as he was led from the parlor by Suffolk's men—an alone young man who would hang before spring came.

She and Dame Perpetua finished Compline's prayers. Quiet closed around them, but neither of them moved. Quiet, even among the cold and shadows, was a blessing just then.

A soft footfall outside the door told them when their respite was past. Frevisse braced herself for whatever demand was coming now, and at the small knock said, "*Benedicite*," in what she hoped was a welcoming voice. From the glance Dame Perpetua gave her, it was not.

Sir Philip entered, carrying another candle. Despite his shielding hand as he crossed the room, its light jumped and fluttered, dancing the shadows around each other until he set it down on the table beside the nuns' small light. He looked around. "No Master Lionel?"

"Gone to his bed, I hope," Frevisse said. "Even he has to give way to the necessities of night."

"As you gave way to Bishop Beaufort's necessity."

So he had not come by chance, but with a need—like her own—to talk about what had happened. But Frevisse could not read his tone to understand his feeling in the matter. She looked at him questioningly. "You'd rather I hadn't done this?"

"I'd rather Jevan had had longer to work through the torments in himself to some sort of better peace. He came to me here yesterday to make confession."

"That's how you knew to stop him from eating the tart."

And why he had not said he had been in talk with Jevan afterwards.

Sir Philip nodded. He looked as tired as she felt, but like her, he could not let the day go yet. "He confessed the murder and his abiding hatred for Sir Clement even after his death, and his hopeless disbelief in God's mercy. Given more time—and now he may not be given the time—he might win free of them and go to his death with a clearer soul."

"Or there might not be enough time from here to the world's end for him to do that." Frevisse did not try to conceal her pain at that. "His wounds were as long as his life."

"And as deep."

"At least you stopped him from killing himself. For murder there can be repentance and a chance for heaven. For suicide, he would have been damned without hope."

"It was his living without hope that drove him to do what he did," Sir Philip said gravely.

Frevisse thrust her hands further up her sleeves, huddling in on herself for warmth against the cold that was more than outward. "I could easily find myself in that sin."

Sir Philip's smile was so slight as to be almost unseen in the candle-lit darkness. "But his grace the bishop will remember you as a good and useful servant for your service to him."

"I'd rather he didn't," Frevisse said curtly. "I'll stay the while that Aunt Matilda needs me. Then Dame Perpetua and I will go back to St. Frideswide's and that, please God, will simply be the end of it."

"Nothing is so simple as it ought to be," Dame Perpetua pointed out firmly.

"Especially justice," Sir Philip added.

"Especially justice," Frevisse echoed. But justice did not seem enough. It answered too few things, and most particularly Jevan's despair that, at the last, had betrayed him more than her attempts to reach the truth. She stood up. "There must be somewhere in this house warmer than here. Let's go there."